Please return this book   Fiction
to kilgraston school library

Nancy Drew®
in
The Mysterious M

Nancy Drew Mystery Stories® in Armada

* For contractual reasons, Armada has been obliged to publish No. 51 onwards before publishing Nos. 45–50. These missing nuimbers will be published as soon as possible.

Nancy Drew Mystery Stories®

The Mysterious Mannequin

Carolyn Keene

ARMADA

1990 .

The Mysterious Mannequin
was first published in the USA in 1970
by Grosset & Dunlap, Inc.
First published in the UK in 1980 by
William Collins Sons & Co. Ltd.

First published in Armada in 1990

Armada is an imprint of the Children's Division,
part of the Collins Publishing Group,
8 Grafton Street, London W1X 3LA

CONTENTS

1

The Hidden Message

Nancy Drew opened the door of her father's office and walked in. He had phoned her to pick him up since his car was in the repair shop.

"Hi!" she said to Miss Hanson, his secretary.

"Hello, Nancy," the woman replied. "Your father will be ready in a few minutes." She gave a little chuckle and pointed to a package on a chair near the door. "That came a little while ago. Looks mysterious."

Nancy's interest was aroused at once. The package was about eighteen inches square and well wrapped. She glanced at the airmail stamps and postmark.

"This is from Istanbul, Turkey!"

The attractive teenage detective leaned down to get a look at the sender's name and address. There was none.

"That's strange," she thought.

Just then Carson Drew, a tall, good-looking man in his late forties, appeared from his inner office. He kissed Nancy, then looked at the package.

"What's this?" he asked. "Hm! From Istanbul. I didn't order anything from there. Nancy, have any of our friends been to Turkey recently?"

Nancy thought for a moment. "None that I can think of."

"Let's open the package. Maybe the sender's name is inside."

Miss Hanson took a pair of scissors from her desk and cut the sealing tape. Inside the wrapping was a Turkish prayer rug, measuring three by five feet.

"How beautiful!" Nancy exclaimed, unfolding it.

The centre section of the new Oriental silk rug had a pale-gold background with a flower design. Its rectangular border was an intricate combination of leaves, vines, and geometric symbols in shades of deep rose, blue and gold.

"It's exquisite," Miss Hanson remarked. "Strange that the sender didn't enclose a card."

Mr Drew continued to stare at the rug. Finally he said, "I'm going to hazard a guess about who sent this. Miss Hanson, do you recall my Turkish-American client Farouk Tahmasp?"

The secretary nodded. "He owned the Turkish rug shop in town and disappeared mysteriously."

"He's the one," the lawyer said. He turned to Nancy. "Farouk's shop was over on Satcher Street, where there's a tailor now. It was a very fine shop and he sold many expensive Orientals. Farouk was accused by customs officials of having smuggled in several valuable rugs. He denied it and came to me for advice.

"I took his case, but before it came up in court, Farouk suddenly vanished. He left a note for me saying he could not stand the disgrace, even though he was innocent. He did not say where he was going and I haven't heard from him since. Too bad, because he does not know that he was acquitted. Someone in Turkey had reported wrong information.'

"What a shame!" said Nancy. Her eyes lit up. "I remember that shop. Didn't he have a mannequin in the window?"

"Yes."

Nancy smiled. "It was about six years ago that I first saw the mannequin. It was a young Turkish lady. She wore pale-blue pantaloons and a long-sleeved cerise blouse. What interested me most was the big white veil that covered her whole head except her eyes and the upper part of her nose."

"That's right," her father agreed. "Women in Turkey were required to wear that type of costume before the country became a republic in 1923. But nowadays most of them wear Western-style dress."

Nancy chuckled. "One time, when I stood looking at the mannequin, I was sure she had winked at me. I kept going back to see if she would do it again, but she never did."

Mr Drew and Miss Hanson laughed. Her father said, "With your imagination I can see how you might think that. By the way, Farouk Tahmasp disappeared nearly two years ago."

"And you think maybe he's in Turkey and sent this rug?" Nancy asked. "Did he owe you legal fees?"

The lawyer shook his head. "That's one of the strange parts of the story. Farouk sent me money before he left. He greatly overpaid me and I have always wanted to send him a refund."

"What happened to the mannequin?" Nancy queried.

Her father said he did not know. "Farouk probably sold her to a shop or museum."

Mr Drew went on to say that according to neighbours, all the rugs in the shop had been loaded on a van and taken away. He said that later he found out a dealer in New York had paid cash for the merchandise.

"So there was no way of tracing Farouk," Nancy remarked.

All this while she had been examining the rug. "Since the sender didn't enclose his name, do you suppose there could be a message for you woven into the pattern? I've heard that years ago in Turkey, secret messages were hidden in rugs."

Mr Drew smiled. "Nancy, I value your hunches. Let's see if we can find something."

They laid the rug across Miss Hanson's desk and the three began to examine the border carefully. No one spoke as their fingers traced flowers, vines, and geometric symbols.

In a few moments Nancy spotted an object hidden among some leaves. "I believe it's a car," she said to herself. She moved a forefinger along the rug and came upon the figures of a man and a little boy.

Nancy looked at it steadily for several moments. Then she burst out, "Here's a clue!" She pointed. "See that car? And the man and boy?"

"Yes," Miss Hanson replied. "Does it mean something?"

"I'm sure it does," said Nancy. "My father's name! Car-son! Carson."

"Why, that's marvellous!" Miss Hanson exclaimed. "But I can't understand why Farouk Tahmasp didn't write his message in a letter."

Nancy suggested that the answer might be found in the rug.

"Dad," she said, "I'm sure there's a whole message for you in the border of this rug. Oh, if we can only figure it out!"

Miss Hanson smiled. "You will."

The three searchers became so intent on their task that Mr Drew suggested that they laid the rug on the floor in order to study it better. It was not long before Nancy found another clue.

"Here's a French word: *trouvez*. It means find."

"Find what?" Miss Hanson asked.

The three did not discover anything more during the next five minutes.

"Nancy," said Mr Drew, "it's time for us to go home."

He folded the rug, wrapped it in the paper, and carried it to Nancy's car.

When the Drews arrived home they were met at the door by the housekeeper, Mrs Hannah Gruen. She was a sweet-looking, motherly person who had helped to rear Nancy since Mrs Drew's death when her daughter was only three years of age.

"Nancy," she said, "those blue eyes of yours are sparkling. What has happened?"

"Another mystery!" Nancy announced. "Come into the living room and we'll show you."

The housekeeper was amazed, not only because the identity of the donor was unknown, but also because a message was beginning to unfold itself in the intricate weaving.

"Hannah," said Nancy, "try your hand at discovering what we are supposed to find."

Mrs Gruen laid the rug on the living-room carpet, got down on her knees, and began a search. Meanwhile, Mr Drew had gone upstairs to make a phone call and Nancy went to wash her hands and give Togo, her terrier, his supper.

When she returned to the living room, Hannah Gruen was sitting back on her heels. "I think I've found something," she said. "Look among these vines here. Do you see a word?"

"Offhand, no," Nancy replied. "It's like a vine ladder, isn't it?"

"Turn it sideways," Hannah suggested.

When she did, Nancy cried out in surprise. Woven in and out of the rungs were several letters. "They spell mannequin!"

Mr Drew walked into the room just in time to hear Nancy's exclamation. "Mannequin? We're to find a mannequin? It must be the one that used to sit in Farouk's shop window."

"That's a big order!" Nancy remarked. "We haven't the least idea where she went to."

Mr Drew put an arm around his daughter. "Nancy, I am assigning you the job of locating her."

"Oh, Dad, what a challenge!" she said, hugging him.

The young detective wondered where to begin. She hoped there were further directions in the rug to give her a clue. As soon as dinner was over, she sat down in the living room with the rug on her lap.

Togo lay beside her. After a while the whole pattern in the rug border became a blur. She had just decided to rest her eyes for a while, when the front doorbell rang. Nancy hastened to the door.

"Hi, Ned!" she said as a handsome, athletic young man walked in. He was Ned Nickerson, who lived in Mapleton, a town a few miles away from River Heights, and dated Nancy regularly. He was a student at Emerson College, where he played football, but during his summer vacation he was selling life insurance.

"Hi, Nancy! Any new mysteries since I last saw you?"

"I'm sure you expect me to say no," she replied with a broad grin, "but I'm going to fool you. I ran into one this afternoon. It's in the living room." She led the way inside.

"A mystery? That rug?" he queried.

"Yes. I'll tell you about it on the way to the airport. We'd better hurry so we won't be late picking up Burt and Dave."

Nancy hurried off to tell her father and Hannah that she and Ned were leaving and would bring their friends Bess and George back to the house, together with their two dates.

Ned stopped first at Bess Marvin's house. The pretty, slightly plump blonde climbed into the car. A few moments later they picked up her cousin George Fayne. The slender, dark-haired athletic-looking girl enjoyed her boy's name, even though many people teased her about it.

"I think you'll have to step on it," George remarked to Ned. "You know how Burt hates waiting."

Ned drove directly to the far end of the row of airport buildings, where passengers from private planes came in. The young people got out of Ned's car and went into the waiting room. No one was around.

"I wonder if the boys will be on time," George said. "You'd think there would be some notice on that bulletin board of incoming flights."

Minutes went by. Ned tried to phone the tower to get information but it did not answer. Restless, the group went outside and paced back and forth, keeping their eyes on the sky. Other private planes came in, but not the one they were looking for. Presently they saw a pilot walking towards them. Ned asked him if he knew anything about the N104TR.

The pilot frowned. "I just heard it's having trouble with the landing gear. It won't let down. And they're low on fuel."

Nancy and her friends gasped. Fearful, Bess cried out, "Oh, they'll crash!"

2

"I Love Her"

Moments later Nancy and her friends saw a small twin-engine plane circling the airport. Sirens began to wail as a crash truck sped out. The runway that had been assigned for the crippled plane was quickly sprayed with foam as a protection against fire.

"Oh, I hope they'll be all right!" Bess said prayerfully.

Ned was tense as he remarked, "I understand the owner is a very good pilot. All we can do is hope for the best."

The four young people watched tensely as the plane began its descent. Bess turned her head away and bit her lip.

The plane soared along at what seemed to be just inches above the runway. Seconds later the craft settled down lightly and sent geysers of foam in all directions as it made contact with the ground.

Then gradually yawing to the right it slid sideways to a stop.

"Thank goodness!" George murmured.

Nancy touched Bess. "They're safe!"

An open truck roared up to the side of the plane to

collect the passengers and the pilot. The runway was far too wet with foam for them to walk on. Dave was the first one to emerge and Bess began to laugh and cry all at the same time.

"For Pete's sake!" her cousin George scolded her. "You'll look a mess by the time Dave gets here."

George's reprimand did the trick. Bess dried her eyes and quickly got out her compact to powder away any telltale tears.

The truck stopped at the building where Nancy and her friends were waiting to let Burt Eddleton and Dave Evans off. Burt was blond and husky; Dave blond but with a rangy build.

Bess was the first one to rush forward. She gave Dave such an overwhelming greeting that he looked embarrassed. George greeted Burt less effusively, but said, "I'm glad you're safe."

"I told Hannah I'd call her when you arrived," Nancy said, "so she can get the snack ball rolling."

Twenty minutes later they were all seated around a huge table in the cosy kitchen. Mr Drew appeared and said hello to the visitors. Presently he excused himself and went back upstairs to his study.

Hannah Gruen had prepared one of her midnight specials – toasted ham-and-egg sandwiches over which she had poured a cheese and tomato sauce. Burt and Dave had never had the treat before. Both declared it was one of the best sandwiches they had ever eaten.

"I'll introduce it to the fellows at Emerson," Dave told the housekeeper.

"Nancy," said Burt, "are you working on another mystery right now?"

"I'm trying to locate a missing mannequin, believe it or not."

Dave laughed. "That's certainly something different. If I recall correctly, you started your detective career hunting for *The Secret of the Old Clock*, and recently we helped you solve the mystery of *The Invisible Intruder*. Boy, that was a tough case!"

Nancy showed her friends the mysterious rug and pointed out the message in it that had been unravelled so far.

"Say, that's clever!" Dave declared.

"Dad and I," said Nancy, "are assuming that the man who sent it is a former client of his named Farouk Tahmasp and that he's now living in Istanbul."

"Did he weave this himself?" George asked.

"Probably not. I think most of the weavers in Turkey are women. But no doubt Farouk designed it and the weaver wasn't aware of the message."

The rug was laid on the living-room floor and the six young people dropped to their knees and searched for further clues in the border. None of them found any and presently Bess began to yawn.

"It's time to go home," she said.

The others agreed. As soon as her friends had gone, Nancy turned out the lights and climbed the stairs to her room.

Directly after breakfast the following morning Nancy and Hannah sat down on the living-room floor to study the rug closely. Tracing each leaf, stem, and geometric symbol was tedious work. In half an hour they had examined only two feet of the design. They had found nothing and stood up to stretch.

"Do you think part of the message could be in the flowers in the centre section of the rug?" the house-keeper said finally.

"It's possible," Nancy replied, "but it would be much harder to disguise it there." She noticed one place that looked like a pond with tall stemmed water lilies, but found no letters or words in that area.

She and Hannah worked diligently and five minutes later Nancy exclaimed, "I love – "

From the doorway a voice asked, "Me? That's great!"

Nancy and Hannah looked up to see Ned standing there. As Nancy blushed, Hannah said to him, "How did you get into the house?"

Ned laughed. "Togo let me in. He knows how to unlock the screen door."

"Well, I'll have to look into that at once," said Hannah as she hurried off to inspect both the front and back doors.

Nancy pointed out the words "I love – " in the border of the rug and suggested that Ned try to locate more of the message.

Ned laughed. "You know, Nancy, I get a big bang out of solving part of any mystery before you do. I'm going to try it now." Painstakingly he studied the leaves, vines, and geometric symbols. All of a sudden he shouted, "I have it!"

"What is it?" Nancy asked.

Proudly Ned said, "The whole sentence reads 'I love her.' I suppose he means the mannequin." Then Ned's face took on a look of disgust. "He can have her. As for me, I'll take a live one any time."

Nancy grinned. "Just the same, I bet you could love a mannequin, too, if it held something valuable."

"Is that what you suspect?" Ned asked.

Nancy shrugged. "One guess is as good as another."

Ned stood up. "Now that I've solved part of the mystery for you, let's go! You haven't forgotten about our trip up the river by motorboat to that unusual bookshop?"

"No indeed," Nancy answered. "In fact, I've been thinking that perhaps I could pick up some interesting books on Turkish rugs."

"Oh, I almost forgot. I brought you a souvenir of your new mystery," Ned interjected, pulling a cellophane-wrapped package from his pocket.

Hannah, coming back into the room, exclaimed, "Smyrna figs!"

"Only now the city of Smyrna is called Izmir," Nancy put in.

The housekeeper sighed. "I wish people around the world would stop changing the names of places. I'm getting worn out trying to learn all those new ones. Istanbul was that city's original name. Then they changed it to Constantinople, and I must say I liked that better. Now they've switched back to Istanbul. It's confusing. So much I learned in school has to be unlearned."

Nancy laughed as she opened the package and

passed round the figs. Hannah took hers to the kitchen, saying she would pack a picnic lunch for the couple. She had been gone no more than two minutes when Nancy and Ned heard her cry out.

"I wonder what happened," said Nancy. She dashed towards the kitchen, with Ned at her heels.

They found Hannah holding one hand over the sink. Blood was dripping from a badly cut finger. She was about to put it under the cold water.

"Stupid of me!" she said. "I was trying to slice roast beef with a bread knife."

Nancy offered to take care of the wound and rushed off for a first-aid kit. While she was putting on antiseptic and bandaging the housekeeper's finger, Ned cut thin slices of the roast beef. He and Nancy finished preparing the picnic lunch, then set off in his car for the river.

"It's early," Nancy spoke up. "Would you mind going via Satcher Street so I can drop into the shop Farouk used to have? Maybe the tailor who is there now knows what became of the mannequin."

Ned stopped in front of Anthony's Tailor Shop and Nancy hurried inside.

"Good morning," she said. "I'm trying to find a mannequin that used to be in the window here."

The tailor merely shrugged his shoulders and shook his head. "Speak only little English," he said with an Italian accent. "I not understand."

Just then a high squeaky laugh came from a dark corner of the shop. Nancy turned and for the first time noticed a wizened-looking old man seated cross-legged on a bench.

As she looked at him, he began to laugh uproariously, slapping his thigh and rocking back and forth.

In a high-pitched voice he said, "You lookin' for Farouk's mannequin? Who do you think you're kiddin'?"

3

Bookshop Clue

Puzzled but intrigued by the strange old man in the tailor shop, Nancy walked towards him.

"Why are you laughing?" she asked. "Didn't the mannequin that used to be in the window belong to Farouk Tahmasp?"

Instead of replying the wizened man pulled up his legs, held his knees in both hands, and rocked in this position without saying a word. But he contined to haw-haw.

Nancy was exasperasted but tried hard not to show it. "You knew the rug dealer Farouk, didn't you?" she enquired.

The old fellow did not answer but continued his uproarious laughter. Nancy concluded he must be senile and she probably would never learn the truth from him. And perhaps he did not know the answers.

She walked back towards the tailor who sat staring in amazement, a needle raised in his right hand. Finally he brought down his arm and went on mending a man's coat he held on his lap.

Nancy asked him slowly, "Who owns this building?"

As the man looked at her helplessly, she said, "You pay rent to somebody for your shop, don't you?"

This time the tailor understood. He smiled in a friendly way and replied, "Curtis Realty Company. Around the corner." he pointed towards a side street.

Nancy thanked him. She decided that at the first opportunity she would go there and find out if anyone at Curtis knew what had become of the mannequin.

"Any luck?" Ned asked as she got into the car.

Nancy shook her head and told him about the funny old man and his strange remark. She and Ned tried to figure out what he had meant but were unable to make any sense out of it.

"I think," said Ned, "he's a kook. Let's forget him."

The couple discussed the other aspects of the mystery until they reached the dock. There they boarded a sleek speedboat which was owned by a friend of Ned's.

"What a beauty!" Nancy remarked.

"Yes, she's pretty cool."

Ned gave the engine full power and it raced along so fast the nose lifted out of the water. The wind blew Nancy's hair out straight behind her.

Ned said he had picked a lovely picnic spot along the Upper River. Nancy tried hard not to miss any of the beautiful scenery along the way or any of Ned's conversation. This ranged from some of his amusing adventures trying to sell life insurance to the organization of the football schedule at Emerson College. But her mind constantly wandered back to the mystery of the mannequin.

Finally Ned realized this and said, "Nancy, if the Farouk case should take you to Turkey, how about letting me go along as your strong-arm man?"

Nancy laughed and did not answer him directly. She said, "Wouldn't it be fascinating to visit Istanbul and see the mosques and the bazaars and the beautiful Bosporus?"

Ned did not reply because at that moment a boat with three twelve-year-old boys, one a reckless pilot, was bearing straight down on them.

"Crazy kids!" Ned muttered as he swerved sharply to avoid the other craft. He yelled at them. "Look where you're going!"

The boys paid no attention. "How about a drag race?" the pilot called out.

"No thanks," Ned yelled.

"Chicken!" the boy shouted and went on.

In a little while Ned pulled towards the shore and docked the boat at a small pier. He picked up the picnic box and helped Nancy out of the boat. They walked along the shore to a small grove of trees and sat down. Both were hungry and enjoyed the delicious lunch of roast beef sandwiches, peaches, and angel cake. As they finished eating, Ned said:

"Tell me, Nancy, what Farouk's mannequin looked like."

"Perhaps I can show you better by making a sketch of her," Nancy suggested.

From her purse she took a sheet of paper and three coloured pencils which she always carried with her.

She worked industriously for a few minutes, then held up the sketch.

Ned grinned. "Groovy picture, but how do you expect me to know what the mannequin looked like with that veil wound around her head and across most of her face?"

"You're right," Nancy replied, laughing, "but all I can do is guess at the rest of her face."

She turned the sheet over and made a completely new sketch. When Nancy finished, the face on the paper that stared up at her looked almost alive. She was a beautiful girl with an oval face framed by long black hair.

"Wow!" Ned exclaimed when she showed it to him. "A real doll! I mean mannequin!"

The couple wondered if by any chance the mannequin could have looked like the face in the sketch. If so, and she was around River Heights, there was a good chance of finding her.

"I'm sure nobody would have destroyed such an attractive mannequin," Nancy remarked. "Well, I'll have to work on that angle of the mystery another day."

She and Ned climbed back into the speedboat and went on up the river until they came to the bookshop. It was a quaint structure with its own docking facilities, where customers tied up their craft and went inside to make their purchases.

As Nancy entered, she said, "What an amazing place! I've never seen so many books in such a small area."

Ned smiled. "The owner boasts that he has a copy of almost every current book and also some that are out of print or rare. I want to pick up two or three volumes in connection with my courses next autumn. Suppose I meet you here at the front door in a little while?"

Nancy nodded and he went off. She began looking around at the rows and rows of books, finally coming to a section on foreign countries. In a few seconds she located a whole shelf of books on Turkey. After choosing one on rugs, she picked up a volume on the history of the country and looked at the table of the contents.

Famous Paşas was the title of one chapter. Nancy turned to that part of the book and soon became absorbed in reading passages about Turkish history in which various *paşas*, men of high government rank, had been involved. Turning a page, she blinked in disbelief. One of the famous men had been named Tahmasp.

"I wonder if Farouk is a descendant of his?" she asked herself. "Maybe Dad could contact a living member of his family and find him that way."

Nancy purchased the book and also another on Istanbul. She went to the front door, but Ned was not there yet. Seeing a pay telephone in the corner of the shop, Nancy called her father and told him what she had read. The lawyer said he would cable the police chief of Istanbul immediately to find out if Farouk Tahmasp or any member of his family lived there.

"I'll tell the chief I have good news for Farouk.

Then, if Farouk gets the message second-hand, he won't feel that he has to hide any longer."

By the time Nancy reached the front door again, Ned was there and she told him of her possible clue. He chuckled.

"I was sure that if I brought you here, you'd learn something useful."

The trip back to River Heights was without incident. Ned remarked, "I'm glad those crazy kids got off the river. I'd hate to see this borrowed boat wrecked."

The craft was secured and Nancy and Ned returned to the Drew house. They found Bess and George there with Hannah Gruen.

At once Bess rushed up to the couple. "Wait until you hear the cool surprise we have for you!"

4

Togo to the Resuce!

"A cool surprise?" Nancy questioned. "Is it in connection with the mystery?"

Bess, George, and Hannah Gruen nodded affirmatively. George said, "We've found another word in the border of the rug."

Nancy smiled. "Don't make me guess what it is. Tell me quick."

"It's in English," Bess spoke up. "The word is 'carry'. See, here it is."

Ned repeated the whole message so far: "'Carson, find mannequin. I love her. Carry –'"

Hannah, Ned, the girls looked at one another, puzzled. What was Mr Drew supposed to carry and where? No one had a ready answer, and Bess and George expressed regret at never having seen the mannequin in the window of Tahmasp's rug shop.

Bess glanced at her wrist watch. "I really must go home," she said. "Nancy, if you learn what the rest of the sentence is, let me know."

George said she must run along too, but Nancy and Ned continued to study the rug. Nancy, recalling that Hannah had a sore finger, decided she should help with the preparations for dinner. She excused herself to go to the kitchen.

Half an hour later Mr Drew came in and soon afterwards dinner was served. Conversation turned to the discovery of the word "carry", but like the others, the lawyer had no idea what the rest of the sentence was.

"It's interesting that Farouk used both French and English in his message," he remarked. "You may find words in other languages, even Greek or Turkish."

Ned laughed. "I'd be sure to miss them. To me the characters look like part of a design rather than a word."

"I hope Farouk didn't use any Greek or Turkish letters of the alphabet. We'd never recognize them."

Directly after dinner Ned said he would have to leave. "I'll be in touch," he told Nancy. "And wish me luck selling a big fat insurance policy to my client."

"I sure do," Nancy said.

Nancy sat down in the living room to read the volume on Turkey which she had bought at the river bookshop. She became engrossed in the descriptions of various interesting places. The Topkapi Palace, she read, had been the home of several generations of sultans but was now a museum. On exhibit in one of the Palace's many buildings were the extravagantly ornamented garments, headpieces, and various objects that had belonged to the sultans and their families.

"Oh my goodness!" Nancy said to herself as she read that the palace had three hundred and twenty rooms and that three thousand people had once lived under its roof. Many of these of course were servants.

"Kemal Ataturk changed all this and made Turkey a republic," Nancy read. "He is considered the George Washington of present-day Turkey."

The book contained many colour photographs. One showed a service of gold coffee cups, each one inlaid with two hundred and forty diamonds. There was an ebony bench inlaid with ivory. A huge turquoise had been embedded in the centre.

"How exquisite!" Nancy said to herself as she gazed upon a cradle of gold inlaid with jewels. She laughed softly. "I wonder if the baby in it slept any better than those in plain old wooden cradles!"

She put down the book and stared into space, visualizing life at the Topkapi Palace long ago. Laughter, music, dancing girls in costume, the magnificently attired sultans.

Nancy suddenly sat up straight and came back to reality. She was reminded of the mannequin who might have looked like one of the sultan's wives.

"I haven't tried to track her down in the River Heights shops that sell women's dresses," Nancy thought, "and I haven't checked the museum!"

The grandfather clock in the hall was just chiming eight.

"The stores and the museum will be open until nine," Nancy told herself, getting up.

She hurried to the hall and consulted the classified telephone directory. One after another she called each department store and dress shop in town. Not one of them had purchased a mannequin from the rug dealer.

Nancy sighed and called the museum. An assistant to the curator answered.

"By any chance," Nancy asked, "do you have a mannequin that came from Farouk Tahmasp's rug shop a couple of years ago?"

"We have one, but I don't know where she came from," the man replied. "She's a Turkish lady wearing a white veil."

Nancy's spirits soared. Had she found Farouk's mannequin? "I'll be right down to see it," she told him.

Nancy quickly explained to her father and Hannah where she was going and rushed outside to get her car.

"Hold on!" her father called. "I'm coming along!"

It was already eight-thirty so Nancy drove at the speed limit. She parked quickly and the Drews rushed into the museum.

"Where's the Turkish mannequin, please?" Nancy asked the guard in the entrance hall.

"Downstairs."

Nancy and her father ran down the steps. Ahead of them was an exhibit of figures in costume from many countries of the world. They hunted for the Turkish figure and finally found her on the far side of the room. Her outfit was different from the one Nancy recalled in Farouk's window. Could she be the mannequin they sought?

The custodian of the exhibit had followed the

Drews. In a rather tired voice he said, "It's nearly nine o'clock, folks. That's closing time."

"I know," said Nancy. "Tell me, where did the museum get this mannequin?"

"Some wealthy woman gave it to us."

"When was that?"

"Oh, about five years ago – maybe longer."

The Drews looked at each other in disappointment. At last the lawyer said, "My daughter and I are looking for a certain Turkish mannequin. This isn't the right one."

Nancy and her father said good night to the custodian and went up the stairs. Neither spoke until they were in the car. Then Mr Drew patted his daughter's shoulder.

"It was a good try, Nancy. Better luck next time."

Mrs Gruen was sorry to learn of their dashed hopes. "Something good is bound to pop up," she prophesied.

Nancy nodded and went back to the big upholstered wing chair in the living room to continued reading the book on Turkey. Togo snuggled beside her.

First Mr Drew, then Hannah stopped to say good night to her, suggesting that she not stay up too late.

The young detective smiled. "One more hour," she said. "This book is absolutely fascinating." Nancy sighed. "It certainly makes me want to visit Turkey."

"I was there once at the time of Ramadan," her father said. "That is the most holy month of the year for the Moslems. During that period they eat nothing each day between dawn and sunset. At the end of the month, the young people follow a very lovely custom. It is called the Sugar Holiday. They buy bonbons and give them to the old people."

Hannah had picked up the prayer rug from the floor and draped it carefully over a chair in the hall. Nearly an hour went by, when Nancy thought she heard someone fumbling at the kitchen door. Apparently it did not bother Togo because he neither barked nor got up.

But when Nancy rose and walked towards the kitchen, Togo followed her. She went through the darkened room and peered outside. There was no one around.

"Perhaps I'd better turn on the porch light," she thought, and flicked the switch.

The outside lamp illumuniated the entire Drew yard. No one was in sight.

"I must have heard a prowling animal," Nancy thought.

She turned off the light and went back to the living room. She became interested in reading that the name of the Moslems' sacred scripture is the Koran.

"Today's students are finding it extremely difficult to read the book because it is not printed in the latinized alphabet being used in the schools."

The author went on to say that a translation was in progress. "Parents are glad it is being done because they believe it is important that their children are able to read the Koran from cover to cover."

Nancy was about to put the book down when she idly turned to a section of colour photographs showing robes and uniforms of olden times when sultans and their assistants lived so lavishly.

"Imagine!" she thought. "This uniform has two hundred and six diamonds sewn into it!"

Nancy finished looking at the fabulous costumes, then turned off the light and sat thinking about the mystery. Presently she was startled again by a sound from the rear of the house. Was someone tiptoeing on the ground floor? She did not move and Togo did not wake up.

A few seconds later the young detective became aware of the shadow of a man moving forward from the rear of the hall. She stood up without making a sound. The intruder sneaked towards the front door, his back to her. He grabbed the Turkish prayer rug from the chair in one hand. With his other he turned the front doorknob.

"Stop!" Nancy cried out, leaping across the living-room floor to the hall.

The thief turned, startled. Nancy reached for the rug and was able to grab one end of it with both hands. The man gave it a yank but she would not let go.

"Don't you dare take this!" she shouted at him, and called loudly, "Dad! Dad!"

By this time the man had the front door partly open. Nancy began to feel she was waging a losing battle until Togo joined her.

Seeing the tug of war, the terrier growled. Then he leapt up the grabbed the man's shirt cuff.

5

Burglar's Bracelet

The tug of war went on. Nancy was fearful that the precious prayer rug would be torn apart or damaged and the rest of the message in its border ruined.

The thief held on to the rug, despite the fact that Togo was clinging to the man's ripped shirt sleeve and Nancy was pulling at the rug. He managed to get outdoors, yanking it with him. Once there, however, he gave up and sped down the driveway.

By this time Mr Drew and Hannah, awakened by the commotion and Nancy's cries, had run down to the ground floor. Togo was chasing the man and barking wildly. When they reached the street, the little dog gave up the chase. But he continued to yap at the disappearing figure until Nancy called him back.

"Good dog!" she said. "You saved the rug."

"What do you mean?" Mr Drew asked.

Nancy told what had happened. While Hannah examined the rug, Mr Drew hurried to the telephone and reported the burglar to the police.

Two officers arrived in a short time. The one named Wolf asked for a description of the intruder.

"He is in his early twenties, of medium height, and

has blue eyes," Nancy reported. "His hair's black and he has a beard and moustache. He could be of Turkish descent."

The officers knew of no such person, but said they would try to locate him. Wolf reported to head-quarters over his short-wave radio, while the other policeman went with the Drews and Hannah Gruen to the rear of the house, hoping to discover how the intruder had entered. The kitchen door and all the windows were locked.

"That burglar is a slick one," Mrs Gruen remarked. "He must have had a master key."

The officer opened the door and examined the lock. "I'd say the fellow has a special kind of master key. No ordinary key would open this." He made several notes in his report book, then he and his partner left.

Soon afterwards, everyone went upstairs. Nancy took the prayer rug with her and hid it in her bedroom cupboard. Just before going to sleep an idea came to the young detective. She would get hold of Bess and George the following morning for a tour of locksmith shops in River Heights and surrounding towns to find a possible clue to the burglar.

Her two friends were amazed to hear what had happened at the Drew home and excited to help Nancy track down the intruder. The three girls drove off in Nancy's car soon after nine o'clock.

The locksmiths in River Heights could not help Nancy. None of them had ever seen a man fitting the description of the Drews' burglar. In several nearby towns the girls had no better luck.

Finally they reached the town of Everest and looked in the classified section of the telephone directory to locate locksmiths. There was only one and Nancy drove directly to the shop. In the window was a sign:

R. S. SMITH
I GUARANTEE TO OPEN ANY UNUSUAL LOCK

Nancy, Bess, and George grinned. George remarked, "That's almost like advertising you're a super-duper burglar."

Bess said in a whisper, "Nancy maybe he is the man you're looking for."

R. S. Smith was a tall, blond, good-natured man who in no way resembled the Drew's intruder.

"Good morning, young ladies," he said. "What can I do for you? I bet you've locked your key in your car!"

The girls smiled and Nancy said, "No, and I'm afraid we have no business for you. We'd like some help, though."

"Shoot!" said the man, leaning across the counter.

Nancy quickly told her story and Mr Smith frowned. "Sounds bad. I believe I can help you at that. A fellow answering your description was in here about a week ago. He said he read my sign in the window and would like to challenge me.

"He bragged that he could open something I couldn't. I took him up and brought out a lock which I admit I've never been able to open. Do you know that within five minutes that guy had it unlocked? He used a master key he carried in a pocket."

"Fabulous," said Bess.

George added, "I'll bet he's the person we're looking for. Have you any idea where he is?"

Mr Smith shook his head. "I asked him if he had a business card with him. He said no. Then he turned on his heel and walked out of here. I can't tell you much else, except I think he's a foreigner – speaks with a slight accent."

"You've been a great help," Nancy said. "Thank you."

She was glad to have obtained that much information, although disappointed not to have the man's name or address. She left her own name and telephone number in case the suspect should come back.

Just as the girls were about to leave, Mr Smith said, "I just thought of something that might help you. While that guy was working on the special lock, one of his sleeves pulled up. I noticed he wore a real fancy bracelet."

"What did it look like?" Nancy asked.

Mr Smith described it as being very wide and made of gold filigree. "It was studded with turquoise," he added, then laughed. "You wouldn't catch *me* wearing anything like that!"

George made a face. "I don't blame you."

Bess disagreed. "Why shouldn't a man wear a bracelet if he wants to?"

Nancy thanked Mr Smith for his help and led the way back to her car.

"It's lunchtime," Bess reminded the others. "I could go for a nice big salad. I saw a sign a few miles back advertising the Water Wheel Restaurant a short distance beyond here. It sounds good. Let's try it."

"Okay," said Nancy, and headed the car in that direction.

The place was picturesque, with tables set in an attractive garden along the water. The river was a rushing millstream with a huge water wheel in full operation.

"How charming!" Bess murmured, getting out of the car. "Let's try to get a table right by the water."

The head waitress complied with her request and led the three girls to a table very near the bank of the rushing stream. Bess's desire for a huge fruit salad was gratified while Nancy and George each took a shrimp salad.

"Do you girls want dessert?" George asked half an hour later. "I'm stuffed."

Before anyone could answer, Nancy's attention was caught by a little boy who was running among the tables. Playfully one of the guests made a grab for him. In dodging out of the way, the child came so close to the edge of the bank that he lost his balance and toppled into the water!

"Oh!" cried Nancy.

She was out of the chair like a shot, kicked off her shoes, and dived in. She knew the little boy would be swiftly carried towards the water wheel and scooped up. His small body would be battered. He might even be killed!

With quick strokes she reached the child's side and held on to him. By this time Bess and George and other guests had come to the edge of the bank and were looking down in horror.

"Hypers!" cried George. "I'd better go in and help!"

The combined strength of the two girls kept them and the boy from being swept closer to the water wheel. They staggered to the side of the stream, where Nancy handed up the child to Bess. Then she and George, grasping vines and jutting rocks, managed to pull themselves to the top.

There were cries of relief and praise from the crowd. The little boy's mother and father had run out from the inside dining room of the restaurant. They tried to quiet the hysterical child.

"How can I ever thank you?" the woman half sobbed.

The father shook hands with each of the dripping girls and said, "You are very brave. God bless you both."

By this time the owner of the restaurant had been summoned. She asked Nancy and George to follow her inside at once and took them upstairs to a bedroom. The woman gave them robes and said she would put their clothes in her electric dryer.

A little later she appeared with the girls' clothes, shoes, and purses. A waitress carried a tray of hot tea. They thanked her and Nancy said she wanted to pay for their lunch checks.

"I guess we've lost our appetite for dessert."

The woman smiled. "The little boy's parents were so grateful they paid for your lunches," she said.

"Both of them felt they should leave and get their son home as soon as possible."

George chuckled. "Kind of a risky way to earn a free lunch!" she remarked.

"Yes," the woman said. "I hope nothing like this ever happens here again."

Bess was waiting for the girls when they came downstairs. Even she had not been tempted to order dessert. "My heart's been pounding from the scare for the past half hour."

She and the others headed for River Heights. Bess and George expected Nancy to take them to their homes, but instead she turned down an unfamiliar side street and presently stopped.

"Where are we going now?" George asked.

"The Curtis Realty Company. It collects the rent from the shop that used to be Farouk Tahmasp's. I want to ask if they know what became of the mannequin."

Bess and George decided to wait in the car. Nancy entered the realty company office. The only one on duty was a smart-alecky young man.

"Looking for an apartment?" he asked with a smirk.

"No," Nancy replied and did not smile back. "The tailor shop on Satcher Street which you are leasing used to be rented by a rug dealer and I – "

"Oh, I remember that guy," the young man interrupted. "Funny fellow. Never laughed."

Nancy thought, "Farouk probably didn't like this wise guy's kind of humour and didn't laugh at it."

"You may recall that he had a mannequin in his

window," Nancy continued. "I'm trying to find out where it is."

"Alex," the young man said, thumping himself on the chest, "Alex would say Farouk buried her in the cemetery."

"The cemetery!" Nancy exclaimed.

Alex gave a wide, sadistic grin. "What would you do with a dummy that you couldn't take with you when you ran away? Suppose you thought too much of her to give her away or sell her? You'd bury her!"

Nancy was stunned by such a thought. She was about to turn and leave, but stopped and said, "Please give me a straight answer. Have you any idea where the mannequin is?"

"No."

When Nancy reached the street, she saw the little tailor running towards her. He looked very excited.

Waving a hand back towards his shop, he said, "Come with me. I help you!"

Turkish Slippers

Nancy beckoned to Bess and George to get out of the car and come with her. She told them what the tailor had said. Curious, the three girls followed him down the street.

"What's the man's name?" Bess asked.

"Mr Anthony."

When they reached the shop, he turned and said, "Today find."

He led the way into the back room where a worn and faded Turkish rug lay on the floor. Mr Anthony scampered over towards one side of the room and turned up a coner of the rug, revealing a wooden floor.

"See something here," the man said and pointed.

The light was rather dim, but the girl's sharp eyes finally detected the bare outline of a large square.

"Is it a trap door?" Nancy asked.

"No understand English trap door," Mr Anthony replied.

He got down on his knees and made an outline of the square with his fingers. Then from his pocket he took a pair of tailor's shears and began to pry up the section of flooring. The girls squatted down and helped him. Presently the square piece was removed.

Below was a shallow area, apparently for storage. Inside lay a pair of women's Turkish slippers. Nancy reached down and eagerly lifted them out.

"How attractive!" said Bess.

The slippers were made of flowered satin in a pattern something like that in the rug Mr Drew had received from Istanbul. The toes curled up daintily.

"These look new," Nancy remarked. "Do you suppose they could have been worn by the mannequin?"

"I'll bet they were," George answered. "I wonder where the rest of her costume is and why her slippers were hidden here."

There was nothing else in the secret compartment, so the wooden section was replaced.

Mr Anthony spoke up. Addressing Nancy, he said, "I hear you a detective. You take." He pointed to the slippers.

"All right," Nancy agreed without hesitation. "But I'll sign a receipt that I have the slippers." After doing this, she added, "By the way, Mr Anthony, how did you know I was at the realty office?"

"I not know. I go to pay store rent."

"A lucky coincidence for me," Nancy said.

Mr Anthony wrapped the slippers. As the girls were about to go out the front door, the strange wizened man who had been there before came in. Recognizing Nancy, he began to laugh noisily in a high-pitched voice. Bess and George looked at each other, then at Nancy who remained calm.

"You found that mannequin yet?"the old man asked.

Without waiting for an answer, he went over to his usual seat, hopped up, crossed his legs and began rocking back and forth, all the while laughing uproariously.

"You want mannequin?" he said. "Ha-ha-ha!"

The girls waited to see if he would say anything more. When he made no further statement, they left the shop.

Out on the sidewalk, George remarked, "He sure is a nut!"

"I guess so," Bess agreed, "but you know the old fellow just might know something. He acts like somebody who has a secret and is enjoying keeping it from everyone else."

Nancy was thoughtful. "If you're right, Bess, I certainly must talk to him again."

George grinned. "I wish you luck. He doesn't strike me as a person who's going to answer a single question you ask him."

After Nancy had dropped the cousins at their houses, she thought about the day's findings. It had been a pretty profitable day and Nancy could hardly wait to tell her father and Hannah Gruen what she had learned.

Neither of them was at home and Nancy decided to wash her hair and have a bath while waiting for them. On her way upstairs, the telephone rang.

"This is Mr Simpson," the caller said. "I'm the father of the little boy who might have drowned today if it hadn't been for your quick action."

"I'm so happy I got him in time," Nancy said. "How is your son?"

Mr Simpson assured her that he was all right and inquired about how Nancy and George were.

"We're fine," Nancy reported. "And thank you very much for paying for our lunches. It certainly was very kind."

"That's the least I could do," Mr Simpson remarked. 'If I can ever be of any help to you, don't hesitate to call on me."

He said he owned a travel bureau in Compton and was calling from his office.

Instantly an idea came to Nancy. "It's just possible you can help me right now. By any chance, did you ever sell a ticket to a Mr Farouk Tahmasp?"

"The name sounds familiar," Mr Simpson replied. "Hold the line a minute. I'll look in my records."

When the travel agent returned to the phone, he said, "Yes, I did sell a ticket to a man by that name two years ago. The address was a rug shop in your town. He went from here to Canada."

"Canada!" Nancy repeatd. "Have you any idea if he might be living there now?"

"Oh, I think not," Mr Simpson said. "His ticket went on to Paris."

"But you have no idea if he went farther?" Nancy queried.

"No, I'm sorry. I gather you're trying to find this Farouk Tahmasp. If I ever hear from him again, I'll let you know."

Nancy told him that she suspected the man was now in Turkey, probably Istanbul.

There was a long pause, then Mr Simpson said, "If you suspect that, and you really want to find him, you might be interested in a trip which my agency is planning to Turkey. It will leave in a few days. My assistant, Mr Randolph, will guide it."

The suggestion excited Nancy.

"I'd love to go if it seems feasible," she said slowly. "I'll have to let you know. How much time do I have?"

"Suppose I send you a copy of our itinerary. It promises to be a fascinating trip," replied Mr Simpson. "But the tour flies out four days from now so you don't have much time to decide."

The man's voice seemed far away as Nancy recalled the thrilling tales she had read of the exotic country. Here, unbelievably, was not only her chance to visit it but also to trace the mysterious sender of the prayer rug!

"Miss Drew, are you there?" Mr Simpson said after a few moments of silence.

"Oh yes," Nancy answered "I'm sorry. My mind is, I'm afraid, already in Istanbul."

"Then you should make the trip," was the good-natured reply.

Nancy laughed and said she would first have to discuss it with her father. She wrote down the address and telephone number of the travel agency, then hung up.

As she showered and washed her hair, Nancy's

imagination took her to the Middle East and back several times. Suddenly she laughed, realizing she had been so busy thinking she had actually given herself three shampoos! Finally, however, the young detective finished her shower and got dressed.

"I almost forgot that the first thing to do is to find the mannequin," Nancy thought. "Farouk didn't ask Dad to come to Turkey to see him. He asked him to bring the figure that used to sit in his window."

As she pondered the situation, Nancy went to the kitchen to start dinner preparations. Mrs Gruen, a methodical person, always wrote down what the dinner menu would be.

Nancy looked on the pad and murmured, "Cream of mushroom soup, lamb chops, french fries, peas, chocolate pie." At the bottom of the sheet was a notation: tomato salad and special dressing.

"I guess I'll begin on the salad," Nancy thought.

She found three plump ripe tomatoes in the refrigerator, which she skinned and sliced. Just as she was arranging them on beds of lettuce, Hannah Gruen arrived.

"Hello, Nancy," she said. "I'm glad you're here to help. It's difficult for me to cut things with this sore finger."

A few minutes later Mr Drew let himself in through the front door and came directly to the kitchen.

"Oh, Dad, I have so much to tell you and Hannah," Nancy said.

"Can you please wait until I have something to

eat?" he asked, grinning. "I'm so starved I couldn't stand any shock."

Within twenty minutes the family was seated at the table and Nancy began her story. Hannah and Mr Drew were intrigued, especially by the travel agancy's trip to Turkey. As soon as dessert had been served, Nancy excused herself from the table.

"I have something to show you both," she said mysteriously and went up to her room.

"Oh no!" she gasped, stepping inside. "Togo, how on earth – ?"

The little dog, perking up his ears, looked at his mistress. Dangling from his mouth was a curled-toed slipper! The paper in which the pair of slippers had been wrapped was in shreds and strewn across the floor.

"You naughty dog!" she scolded and he dropped the slipper.

Quickly Nancy picked up the mate and gathered the scraps of paper. Neither slipper had been damaged and with a sigh of relief Nancy returned to the dinner table carrying them.

"Bess and George and I are sure these were worn by the mannequin," she said.

Mr Drew looked at the slippers closely, turned them over, then went off for a magnifying glass.

"These shoes have been walked in," he declared. "Not much, though."

Hannah Gruen spoke up. "Maybe the mannequin was too heavy for Farouk to carry and he shoved her along the floor."

"If he did that," said Mr Drew, "it means that he must have taken her in and out of the window. But why?"

The housekeeper had a practical answer. "Perhaps to change the costume or to clean the one she wore."

The lawyer nodded. "That's a very good guess. You're probably right."

The idea of the mannequin being moved in and out of the window intrigued Nancy. She decided that the following day she would ask shopkeepers and residents of Satcher Street what they knew about it.

7

Sly Suspect

After dinner Mr Drew called the police department to enquire if they had learned anything about the burglar who had tried to steal the prayer rug. After a somewhat lengthy conversation, he put the phone down and relayed a disappointing message to Nancy.

"No leads at all on that man who tried to steal the rug," he said. "Chief McGinnis thinks the fellow has probably left town."

"That's too bad," said Nancy. "I keep wondering if he'll make another attempt to get into this house. Dad, I notice you had special burglarproof locks put on both the front and back doors."

"Yes," her father replied. "I'll give you and Hannah keys. But anybody as clever as that fellow can probably figure out a way to unlock them."

The Drews agreed that there was no use worrying about it. They would not live in fear.

Nancy's father asked, "Have you found any more clues in the border of the rug?"

"No, but I think I'll work on it a little right now."

She went upstairs to her room, brought the rug into the living room, and laid it on the floor. Nancy moved a lamp close, showing up the design clearly. For some time there was silence in the room as the young detective and her father, sitting on the floor, endeavoured to find another clue.

"This is frustrating," Mr Drew remarked half an hour later. He grinned. "I admit I'm getting a bit stiff sitting in this position. I think I'll walk around outdoors a little. Want to come along, Nancy?"

"You bet," she said eagerly.

From earliest childhood Nancy had been thrilled whenever her father had said, "Let's take a walk." She had learned a good deal about trees, shrubs, flowers and birds from him.

As they walked along the darkened street, Nancy said, "I hear an owl."

"That's right," her father agreed. He chuckled. "Hear what the wise old one is saying?"

Nancy listened, then she giggled. "It sounds as if he were saying, 'You will, you will!'"

"Exactly," Mr Drew said. "I'll bet when we get back to the house you'll discover another part of Farouk's message."

Nancy squeezed her father's arm. "Are you tired of walking?" she asked with a grin. "I can hardly wait to search the rug for more clues."

Father and daughter laughed and circled several adjoining side streets. Finally they returned to the house. Nancy sped into the living room and dropped to the floor. She again scrutinized the border of the rug. To Nancy's delight her father's prediction came true. She found two more words: "her to."

"Oh, Dad, you were right!" she called out.

The lawyer walked in and looked. "Now the instructions are 'Carson, find mannequin. I love her. Carry her to —' But where?"

Nancy continued her search until she became sleepy, but found nothing. She folded up the rug and took it to her bedroom.

Early the next morning she telephoned George, then Bess. George was already up but Bess sounded very sleepy.

"Want to help me with some sleuthing?" Nancy asked. Both girls said yes, but Bess begged for a full hour to get ready.

"No hurry," said Nancy. "We're just going downtown in the vicinity of the tailor shop and asking people who live or work there what they may know about the mannequin."

Nancy once more took out the rug and began to study it. She had barely begun when the front doorbell rang and Hannah admitted George.

"I decided to walk over and save Nancy the trip to my house," she said.

"Nancy's upstairs," said the housekeeper. "Go right up."

George joined Nancy in the search for further words or symols. A few minutes later she said, "I think I've found something! It looks like 'nst.'"

Nancy stared at the section to which George was pointing. She smiled.

"You're absolutely right. I wonder if it's part of a

word. And also, is it French or English or something else?"

The two girls continued the search. It was several minutes before George found two more letters *le*.

Nancy sat back on her heels, trying to figure out if there was any connection between the two groups. She could think of nothing. Finally she took paper and pencils from her desk for herself and George.

"Let's try to decipher this thing," she said.

Nancy sat at her desk and George at the dressing table. Using the letters *nst* and *le* they tried to make a word. Every few minutes they would heave sighs of disappointment. But suddenly Nancy gave a shout.

"I have it!" she said.

"What is it?" George asked.

"Constantinople!"

George stared at the young detective in admiration. "That used to be the name of Istanbul!"

"Exactly." Nancy began dancing around the room in exuberance. "The mannequin is to be taken to Istanbul!"

The news was too good to keep. As George hurried downstairs to tell Hannah Gruen, Nancy telephoned her father.

"That's great!" he said, then chuckled. "Nancy, it begins to look as if you might have to go to Istanbul."

"And you too," she said.

"We'll see about that," he replied. "Farouk is certainly guarding his secret well. It was clever of him to use letters from the old name of Istanbul as a disguise."

By this time an hour had passed. Nancy and George got into the convertible and went to pick up Bess.

"Hi, sleepyhead!" George greeted her cousin. "You missed all the excitement."

"Tell me about it," Bess begged.

Upon hearing of the message to bring the mannequin to Istanbul, her eyes popped wide open. "Are you going?" she asked Nancy.

"How can I? I don't have the mannequin and I have no idea where she is. By the way, the father of the boy we saved runs a travel agency and has arranged a trip to Turkey."

George grinned. "When do we start?"

There was no more conversation until the girls reached Satcher Street. Then Nancy suggested that they separate to make enquiries about the mannequin. She would take the centre section, while the girls enquired at the two ends.

Nancy spoke to the shopkeepers on either side of Mr Anthony's shop. Both said they had moved there after Farouk had left, and knew nothing about his business.

The young detective went across the street to interview shopkeepers there, but had no better luck until she went into a bakery. The owner said he could not help her, but he was sure that Mrs Beimer, who occupied an apartment above his shop, would be able to give her some information.

"She's lived in this neighbourhood for many years."

Nancy rang the bell of Mrs Beimer's apartment and a pleasant-looking woman came to the door. The girl smiled and said she was trying to find the mannequin that used to be in Farouk Tahmasp's window. "Have you any idea where she was taken?"

Mrs Beimer shook her head. "Please come in," she said and led the way to her living room. She motioned Nancy to a chair near a front window.

In the conversation that followed, Nancy learned that the mannequin had never been left in the window overnight and at times it did not even appear in the daytime. Her costume was often changed.

"I thought this might be some kind of Moslem custom," Mrs Beimer said.

"Have you any idea," Nancy asked, "where Farouk Tahmasp went?"

"No. The whole thing happened so suddenly everyone around here was puzzled. We assumed that the rug dealer had taken the mannequin with him. No one knew why he had left. Although he seemed to have no particular friends, he was a nice person. I understand he didn't owe anyone a cent when he left."

The woman sighed. "I sometimes think he got homesick and went back to his native land.'

Since Mrs Beimer could not provide any further information about Faouk, Nancy changed the subject. "Do you know who the humorous old man is who spends a lot of time in the tailor shop? The one who laughs a lot?"

Mrs Beimer grinned. "Oh, I know who you mean. He's half cracked, but sometimes he hits the truth in what he says."

"What's his name?" Nancy asked.

"His last name is Hyde and his nickname is Haw-Haw. He likes to be called that."

Mrs Beimer warned Nancy to be careful of telling Haw-Haw anything she did not want passed along. "He's a great gossip."

Nancy stood up. "Mrs Beimer, I appreciate all this information."

She happened to glance out the window and gasped. A young man lounging in a doorway across the street was the Drews' burglar!

Nancy hurriedly said goodbye to Mrs Beimer and ran down to the street. Knowing that it would be unwise to confront him alone, the young sleuth went into the bakery and asked the owner to telepone the police.

"In the meantime I'll trail the suspect if he leaves."

The baker was very glad to cooperate. Nancy watched from inside. The man in the doorway suddenly started up the street at a brisk pace.

Nancy turned to the baker. "Please ask the police to follow me up the street."

Nancy dashed to the sidewalk and hurried after the young man. She wondered if he was wearing a gold filigree bracelet studded with turquoise.

He began walking so fast that it was almost a run. Nancy was still nearly a block behind. Between milling pedestrians and heavy traffic she had a difficult time keeping him in sight. Fortunately he did not turn any corners.

"Oh, I hope the police will hurry!' she said to herself.

At that moment the suspect stopped abruptly. A young woman coming up a side street also stopped. Nancy noticed that she was very pretty and had long black hair.

The man whipped a letter from a pocket and handed it to her. She opened it quickly and read the message, which apparently was short but disturbing. She burst into tears.

"It really must be bad news," Nancy thought.

She continued to move closer, but at a slower pace in order to see more of the drama. The young man put an arm about the girl and drew her to him. She pushed him away and shook her head violently. He tried again. This time she used her fist against his chest to shove him away.

Nancy was so intent on the scene that she had not noticed a car coming up alongside her. Now she turned to look at it. The police! And Bess and George were in the rear seat.

"What's up?" George called out.

At that instant the Drews' burglar spotted Nancy and the police. He said something to the girl with him. They turned in opposite directions and fled along the side street.

"Bess and George, follow that girl!" Nancy said. "The police and I will go after the burglar!"

8

Shocking News

Bess and George jumped from the police car and sped down the street after the fleeing girl. Nancy stepped into the rear seat and the driver took off after the Drews' burglar. A block farther on he dodged into an office building.

One of the officers turned to Nancy. "You stay in the car and blow the horn if you see the man. We'll go into the building and investigate, okay?"

Nancy nodded, though disappointed she could not continue the chase herself.

The policemen disappeared inside while Nancy kept an alert look on all the buildings. It occurred to her that the suspect might go to the roof, jump to the next building, and make his way to the street again unseen.

"That fellow wouldn't dare show himself here now," Nancy decided. "I'll get out of the car so I can see better."

She walked along the sidewalk and stared upward. Several passers-by paused to look also.

"Somebody up there?" a man asked Nancy.

"I don't know, but the police are looking for a man who ran into that building."

More people stopped until a good-sized crowd had focused their eyes on the rooftops. Nancy was sure that if the suspect were up there, someone would spot him. She decided to watch the jewellery and clothes shops on either side of the office building in case he should run out of one of them.

The crowd of onlookers attracted the attention of Bess and George, who had searched in vain for the burglar's acquaintance. As they rushed up to see what had happened, Nancy caught a glimpse of the suspect. He was just emerging from a drugstore a little farther down the street.

Instantly Nancy said, "Bess, blow the car horn and keep blowing it until the police come back. Then follow me. George, come along!"

Taking deep breaths, the girls started after the man. Within seconds there was a din on the street. The shrill siren of the police car kept wailing. People shouted and pointed towards Nancy and George who were running at top speed down the street. The burglar looked back. Seeing the girls racing after him, he doubled his pace.

Nancy and George ran faster, but the distance between them and the fugitive remained the same.

"Look!" Georg panted.

The suspect was pulling a wallet from the back pocket of his trousers. He brought both hands in front of him and evidently took something from the wallet. Then he returned it to the pocket. Within seconds the wallet popped out and dropped to the sidewalk. The suspect apparently did not know he had lost it because he did not wait to retrieve the wallet.

Nancy and George ran even faster. Nancy scooped up the wallet and yelled at the man. "Stop! You lost your wallet!"

She was sure he had heard her but he paid no attention and sped on.

"Nancy, it's no use," George called to her friend, who was a few paces ahead.

"Don't give up now!" Nancy replied.

George, loyal to Nancy, ran faster. The girls tried their best to overtake the man. He suddenly cut across a parking lot filled with cars. Presently he dodged behind a small truck and they could not see where he went. Unfortunately there was no fence round the place, merely a barrier about a foot high.

"I'm afraid he's gone," Nancy said.

Nevertheless, the two girls scurried in and out among the cars and looked beyond the barrier, but could not see their quarry anywhere. Finally they gave up the chase and returned to the street.

At the same time Bess arrived with the police. Nancy told her story and one of the men said, "That fellow sure acts as if he's guilty of some crime."

Nancy handed the wallet to the officer who said his name was Parker.

'Hm! All identification has been removed."

Nancy was sorry to hear this. She had been hopeful of finding out who the suspect was.

"There's nothing in here but a letter without an envolope," Parker remarked.

He unfolded the sheet and stared at the writing. Nancy looked too.

"Is that in Greek?" she asked.

"Is it?" Parker asked his companion. When he said yes, Parker introduced him as Officer Paras of Greek descent.

"Will you translate this for us?"

Paras read it through silently, then said, "The handwriting is rather poor but I think it says, 'I made an investigation here in Istanbul. Farouk Tahmasp is dead.' It is signed Seli."

"Dead!" Bess shrieked.

The two officers looked at her in amazement and Parker asked, "You know this Farouk?"

"No, not personally," Bess answered. "Nancy Drew here will tell you about it."

Without revealing all the angles of the mystery, Nancy said, "He was a cleint of my father's before he disappeared. We have been trying to find out something about him."

Officer Paras said, "I guess this note answers your question."

Nancy did not contradict him but a sudden suspicion had entered the young detective's mind. "May I see the note, please?"

The officer handed it to her. She scrutinized the paper carefully, then held it up to the bright sunlight. She was not surprised to find that it had been manufactured in the United States.

"See something?" George asked her.

Nancy revealed what she had discovered, and

added, "I believe this letter is a fake. It was written to make the girl he was talking to think that Farouk is dead."

George interposed, "But why would this guy write the letter in Greek of all things?"

"Maybe he's Greek," Bess said simply.

Nancy did not enter into the cousins' conversation. Instead she gave a more detailed account of the whole episode to the police officers, including the fact that the girl, after reading the letter, had burst into tears.

"The man seemed to be trying to soothe her but she kept repulsing him. Then when he saw me, he told her to run and not be caught. He went in the other direction."

"The whole thing does look fishy," Parker admitted.

Bess burst out, "What a terrible trick to play on anyone!"

"Do you suppose," said George, "that the girl the burglar met is a relative of his or possibly of Farouk Tahmasp?"

"She could be," Parker answered.

He asked Nancy for a description and said the police would look for her. "Perhaps if she learns the note is a fake, she'll reveal the identity of the man who showed it to her."

Paras added, "If we find out anything at all, we'll be in touch with you."

The two men drove off. Nancy, Bess, and George returned to the convertible.

"It's certainly been an exciting morning," Bess remarked. "When we saw you run out of that bakery, we rushed. The police arrived. We told them we were working with you and they took us along.'

George observed, "Well, we got one new clue in the mystery. That the suspect is connected in some way with Farouk. He must know Farouk sent the rug. I wonder if the burglar is a Turk or a Greek."

"He could be a Greek who lived in Turkey," Nancy replied. "When I first saw him in our house, I thought he might be Turkish."

A large clock in a jeweller's window told the girls that it was lunchtime. Bess suggested that they all went to her house.

"I'll make one of those fluffy cheese soufflés," she said.

Nancy smiled. "It sounds good, but an idea just came to me of how we might do a little more sleuthing."

Bess groaned. "I vote for it if it includes food."

George looked at her cousin in disgust. "You and your appetite! How about our going to a diet restaurant?"

Nancy laughed. "Not today. I know of a wonderful restaurant in the section of town where most of the people speak Greek.'

George said she knew the one Nancy meant. "It has an odd name, Akurzal Lokanta. It's been there for a long time and the food's delicious."

"Lokanta is the Greek word for restaurant," Nancy added. "Akurzal must be the owner's name. I thought we might have lunch there and possibly pick up some information."

Bess was delighted with the idea until Nancy brought up a new subject. As they were driving towards the restaurant, she said, "It's just possible that burglar dropped the wallet on purpose to mislead us."

"I agree," George said. "First he removed all the contents except the letter, so he couldn't be identified."

A worried expression came over Bess's face. "Nancy," she said, "if he'd do that, maybe even that little drama of the girl crying was part of the act."

"You're probably right," her cousin said.

Bess looked frightened. "Nancy, I don't think we should go to the Greek restaurant. Suppose that awful burglar decides to have lunch there too? Oh, Nancy, I have a feeling you'll be in real danger if you go there!'

9

Silent Warning

George looked at Bess and said, "You know perfectly well Nancy wouldn't give up the case. She's not a scaredy-cat."

Bess defended herself. "It's not a matter of being scared. I think Nancy's in danger."

As often happened Nancy had to play the part of peacemaker between the cousins. Now she said, "Probably you're both right. But I'm sure nothing is going to happen to any of us while eating in that Greek restaurant. It's a perfectly respectable part of town, even though it is old and some of the buildings are a bit shabby."

"And besides," George put in, "I bet there's more than one Greek restaurant in town. The burglar has a choice."

"Oh, all right," Bess conceded. "Next you'll be telling me there are zillions of Turkish restaurants there."

As the girls rode along, conversation turned to the subject of the mannequin.

"Do you really think," George asked Nancy, "that Farouk hid something in her and that's the reason he wants her brought to Istanbul?"

"Your guess is as good as mine," she answered. "I admit I'm puzzled."

"If he did," George went on, "why didn't Farouk take whatever it was with him?"

"Yes," Nancy added, "and why would he ask my father to bring the mannequin to Istanbul? Why not have it sent? And why did he ask my father? Why not a relative or a close friend?"

George had an answer. "You said Farouk left because he thought he was going to be indicted for smuggling and couldn't stand the disgrace. He would have travelled as lightly as possible, not taking any baggage at all from here. He probably planned to purchase new clothing in Canada before flying to Paris."

Nancy smiled. George's reasoning made sense. She answered, "I can only guess that he did not trust anyone except my Dad."

Bess had been listening without comment. Now she said, "I have one great big why. Why did Farouk make everything so complicated? He sure must be scared of something or somebody."

By this time they had entered the narrow street where the Akurzal Lokanta was located. Nancy had to drive some distance up the block before she found a parking space.

On the walk to the restaurant the girls were intrigued by the foreign-looking shops along the way. Tall, narrow-necked coffeepots were among the many attractive objects made of brass. Bess especially liked the leather hassocks and large silk pillows to be used for sitting on the floor.

She gave a little giggle. "Don't let me loose here. I'll be spending more money than I can afford. Aren't the things yummy?"

George could not resist the temptation to tease her cousin. "But think of all the work keeping that brass polished!"

The girls entered the restaurant and were assigned a table. The place was well filled and waiters were bustling around. When one came to take their order, all three girls said they would have vine leaves stuffed with meat, and baklava for dessert.

While Nancy was waiting, she looked around at the diners, wondering if any of them might be able to answer her questions about Farouk or the Drews' burglar. Presently a short, stout man came from the kitchen and paused at her table.

Smiling, he said, "Pardon, miss. But I think I have seen your picture in the newspapers. Are you not Miss Nancy Drew the detective?"

"Yes, I am," Nancy replied modestly.

She had noticed that people at nearby tables apparently had heard the question and were looking in her direction. She requested the man to sit down, saying she would like to ask him a few questions.

"These are my friends, Bess Marvin and George Fayne."

The man bowed and replied he was Mr Akurzal, owner of the restaurant. He said to Nancy, "How can I help you?"

She told him they were looking for two people who, they thought, might be either Greek or Turkish. "One is a young lady. She's beautiful and has big dark eyes and long black hair."

The restaurant owner smiled. "Most Greek and Turkish girls are beautiful."

"The other person," Nancy went on, "is a young man in his early twenties. He has blue eyes, black hair, and a moustache and beard."

Before Mr Akurzal could reply, a man at a nearby table jumped up and came towards the table. He was about forty years of age, swarthy, and had narrowed eyelids. He began waving a fist at Nancy.

"Why are you asking all these questions?" he demanded.

Bess looked frightened and George sat ready to take Nancy's part should there be any trouble.

Nancy herself remained calm. "Suppose you introduce yourself," she said coldly.

The belligerent man stopped waving his fist and turned to the owner.

"If you tell these girls anything, you have me to reckon with!" he shouted.

Mr Akurzal, looking very embarrassed and uncomfortable, rose. "I must attend to something in the kitchen," he said hurriedly and left the room.

The swarthy man glared at the girls but said no more. He returned to his table and did not look in their direction again.

George whispered, "What was all that about?"

Nancy shrugged. She surmised that the obnoxious

man was some kind of a neighbourhood boss. Having overheard that Nancy was a detective, he figured she might be snooping to find out something which he did not want known. Did he know the burglar? She would report the incident to Chief McGinnis.

Bess said in a low voice, "Let's get out of here!"

"I'm sure we're perfectly safe," Nancy reassured her. "Besides, we have already given special food orders. It wouldn't be fair to Mr Akurzal to walk out."

A few minutes later the swinging doors to the kitchen opened and their waiter returned carrying a tray laden with chunks of Greek bread and bowls of yoghurt.

Bess was about to say she had not ordered this, when the waiter said, "The yoghurt is compliments of the house. Make it special here."

As the man went off, a smile crossed Bess's face. "I guess the owner is trying to make up for what happened."

She dipped her spoon into the yoghurt and declared it was delicious. As soon as the girls finished eating it, the waiter brought in the plates of stuffed vine leaves. As he set Nancy's portion down in front of her, he unobtrusively dropped a note into her lap.

She gave no sign that she had noticed it, but instantly spread the paper out on her lap and read it.

"*There are many young people who answer your description but you might look for two men, Cemal Aga and Tunay Arik, and girls, Alime Gursel and Aisha Hatun.*"

Nancy was thrilled by these clues. Mr Akurzal had

undoubtedly written the note and told the waiter to pass it to her without anyone noticing. She slipped the message into her purse and began eating. The main dish was delicious as well as the dessert which followed.

Bess had never had baklava before and was intrigued by the layers of flaky crust baked with honey and filled with chopped nuts. "Absolutely divine," she said.

Mr Akurzal did not reappear in the dining room, no doubt because the unpleasant diner was still there. The girls paid the bill and rose to leave. As they passed the table where the man sat, he glowered at them. Nancy wondered if this was a silent warning to her to stay out of the area.

"But I'll come if I want to!" she told herself.

Nevertheless, Nancy decided to consult her father before hunting up the people named in the note. After the girls were in the car, she told them about her latest clues.

"That's great," said Bess, "but I hope you're not going to start looking for them right now. Haven't we all had enough sleuthing for one day?"

Her cousin agreed. "Nancy, I have a suggestion. You'll put your think machine out of business if you keep up this intense work. Why don't we get hold of Helen Archer and have a good game of tennis?"

Nancy had to admit that she had been pushing on the case since early morning and told the girls she thought it best to talk to her father anyway before continuing her search.

"A few sets of doubles sounds cool. Let's stop at a street phone and call Helen."

She drove to the next corner and George hopped out to make the call. Helen Corning had been married only a short time ago to Jim Archer. She had helped Nancy solve a few mysteries.

George came back to report that Helen would meet them at the club. The girls went home to pick up their tennis gear and within half an hour were batting practice balls back and forth over the net. Presently they were playing in earnest.

After four sets, with Bess and George winning two of them and Nancy and Helen the other two, the four girls sat down to rest. The pretty, brunette bride enquired what mystery Nancy was working on.

When she heard about the mannequin she said, "Oh, I remember her well. Mother used to take me into Farouk Tahmasp's shop once in a while. She loved Turkish rugs. We all wondered what became of him."

She smiled broadly, then went on, "So you're trying to find the mannequin now and take her to Istanbul. How exciting!" Suddenly Helen exclaimed, "Nancy, I believe I know where the mannequin is!"

10

Exasperating Search

Helen Archer's announcement startled Nancy, Bess, and George. In one breath they asked, "Where? Where is the mannequin?"

"Over in the town of Croston. As soon as we shower and change our clothes I'll take you there."

Half an hour later the four were on their way to the river resort town. Helen pulled off the main highway and took a side road up a steep, wooded hill. At the top she parked in front of the beautiful hotel Beauregarde which overlooked the water. She led the girls through the elegantly furnished lobby and down a carpeted hallway to an attractive shop.

"There she is!" Helen said.

In a corner of the shop window stood a Turkish woman mannequin. She was dressed in a costume similar to the one that had been in Farouk's place.

"How exciting!" Bess burst out. "Nancy, I believe your search has come to an end."

Nancy was hopeful but not as positive as Bess.

The glint in the eyes of this mannequin was strangely different from Farouk's. She would soon know the truth.

The four girls walked inside and were greeted by a young boy.

"May I help you?" he asked.

Helen answered, "I'm Mrs Archer. We'd like to talk to the owner."

The boy went off and presently a stylishly dressed, grey-haired woman came from an office.

"How do you do, Mrs Archer?" she said. "It's good to see you again."

Helen introduced her friends to the woman, whom she addressed as Miss Lucille. She said, "Nancy is trying to locate a certain mannequin. I thought the one in your window might be it."

Nancy asked where the woman had purchased her model.

She answered promptly, "Oh, I didn't buy her. All the figures that were for sale didn't please me, so I had this one made to order."

Helen laughed. "Well, Nancy," she said, "I did my best."

"You certainly did and I appreciate it." Nancy turned to the shop owner. "I'm trying to locate a mannequin which used to be on display in the window of a Turkish rug dealer in River Heights. By any chance, do you know the one I'm talking about?"

"Oh yes," replied Miss Lucille. "You are referring to Mr Tahmasp's store?"

Nancy nodded and Miss Lucille continued, "That was a very fine shop. I used to buy rugs from Mr Tahmasp and sell them here."

"Have you any idea what happened to him or his mannequin?" Nancy enquired.

The woman shook her head. "As I recall, the man disappeared rather suddenly. Too bad. He certainly had beautiful things to sell." She paused a moment, then added, "As far as the mannequin is concerned I'm afraid I can't help you. Perhaps you should check with the museums or other stores."

Nancy said she had investigated nearly every possibility without success.

Miss Lucille pointed to a pile of Oriental and American magazines on a table. "There is an article in one of those that might be of some help to you," she said.

At that moment the telephone rang and she excused herself. Bess offered to locate the right magazine. In turning quickly, her arm brushed against a small porcelain bowl on a table. It sailed through the air. Bess, unable to rescue it, closed her eyes as the bowl smashed to bits against the counter.

"Oh!" she wailed. "I'll pay for it, of course, but I'll bet it'll cost me a mint of money!"

Nancy and George thought so too. Helen went over and picked up a few of the pieces. She looked at the name of the maker painted on the botton.

"You're lucky, Bess," she said. "Fortunately this isn't an expensive piece." She continued to look and finally found a fragment with the price tag on it. "It's only five dollars."

"Thank goodness,"said Bess. She opened her purse and took out a note.

Nancy had gone over to the pile of magazines. She came upon part of an old one. It contained an article about dealers of fine Turkish rugs in the United States. She quickly opened the magazine. Staring at her was a photograph of Farouk's shop window with the lovely mannequin seated in the corner.

"Just as I remember her," Nancy told herself. "The eyes are the way I sketched them. Girls, take a look."

By this time they had picked up the pieces of the broken bowl and Bess had paid the clerk the five dollars.

They all stared at the photograph while Nancy thumbed through the article to find the section about Farouk. Unfortunately she did not learn anything new about him, and the names of the magazine, the author, and the photographer had been torn off.

All the girls except Bess made a few purchases, then said goodbye to Miss Lucille and left for River Heights.

As Nancy, Bess, and George were transferring to Nancy's car, Helen laughed. "Bess and George, we didn't succeed, despite our tennis match, in getting Nancy's mind off the mystery!"

"But I enjoyed the game immensely," Nancy insisted.

"Well, lots of luck in finding the mannequin," Helen said as she waved goodbye.

When Nancy arrived home she found Ned there, lying on a porch chaise. "Life at summer camp when I was a counsellor was never like this insurance work," he said, getting up. He explained that he had been trying to sell a policy to a couple in River Heights. "They were hard to get but I sold 'em!" he grinned.

"Good for you," said Nancy.

Ned told her he had dropped in to learn if there were any new developments in the mystery. Hannah Gruen invited him to stay to dinner and he had accepted. Mr Drew drove in right after Nancy and she brought everyone up to date on the latest happenings.

"After dinner, will you men go with me to call on the people whose names the restaurant owner gave me?"

Both said they would like to go, then Mr Drew added, "I have some news of my own. Today I received a cablegram from the chief of police in Istanbul. He had no leads on Farouk Tahmasp."

"Just the same he must be there or in the outskirts of the city," Nancy said.

At dinner she asked if the others agreed about the note in the wallet being a hoax. Hannah suggested that American manufactured paper might be sold in Istanbul and Ned said the Drews' burglar could have sent a gift of letter paper to his friend Seli.

"Possibly," said Mr Drew, "but I'm inclined to agree with Nancy. And don't forget this. The note may not have been the one he showed the girl. But if it was, our burglar must have had a good reason for wanting her to think Farouk is dead or is supposed to be."

Mrs Gruen sighed. "It's certainly confusing."

Ned had been staring into space. Now he said,

"None of this explains why the girl ran in the opposite direction to the one the man took nor what all this has to do with the mannequin."

As soon as they finished dinner, the housekeeper insisted that the others started their search at once. "I'll take care of the food and dishes. My finger is all right now."

Nancy went to get the telephone book and looked for the name Aga. She jotted down the address. Nancy also found Gursel, but neither Arik nor Aisha Hatun was listed.

Mr Drew suggested that since it was such a hot night they should take his air-conditioned car and he would drive.

"Sounds good," said Ned.

All three got into the front seat and started off. Presently Nancy said, "I don't think we should tell these people that Mr Akurzal gave me their names." The men agreed.

Ceman Aga's apartment was easy to find. As the callers went up the stairs to it they wondered if he would prove to be the burglar.

Mr Drew rang the bell and the door was opened by a clean-shaven, dark-eyed young man. He looked surprised but smiled in a friendly way.

He definitely was not the burglar!

"You wish to see me?" Aga asked. He spoke with a foreign accent.

Mr Drew replied they wished to ask him a few questions. "Are you from Turkey?" he queried.

"Yes, Istanbul. I left there a year ago."

"Did you know a Farouk Tahmasp there?"

Aga shook his head. The he said that he had met people by the name of Tahmasp at a seaside resort in Turkey and possibly they were relatives.

"Do you have their address?" Nancy spoke up.

"Once more the young man shook his head. He was sorry.

Mr Drew enquired if Aga knew the three other people they were trying to find and gave their names.

He replied, "I know few people here. It is unfortunate but I cannot help you."

The callers thanked Aga and left.

Alime Gursel lived a few blocks away. Nancy suggested that they went there next.

Ned whispered to Nancy and her father, "I think we're being followed, but every time I turn round the person walks in the other direction. Maybe I'm mistaken."

The three went on and once Nancy looked back suddenly to see if anyone were directly behind them. There were so many people on the street it was hard to decide whether anyone might be following them. Finally she and the others reached the car and climbed in.

Mr Drew started off, the car windows tightly closed because of the air-conditioning.

"It's a relief to get back in here," Ned remarked. "Hot, *très* hot is the word for outside."

The words were hardly out of his mouth when something came whizzing through the air and smashed against the window alongside Mr Drew. The glass shattered!

11

Ah-ee-sha

The rock crashed through the splintered car window, missing the lawyer's head by inches, and fell at Nancy's feet.

Mr Drew stopped the car at once and jumped out, followed by Ned and Nancy. They looked all around for the stone thrower but there was no one in the immediate vicinity.

The noise soon attracted a number of local residents, who demanded to know what had happened.

"Someone threw a stone at my car," Mr Drew explained. "He might have injured me or my daughter or this young man here. If any of you can help find out who he is, I'd appreciate it."

The men, women, and children who had gathered looked at one another but said nothing. Were they covering up for the guilty person? Or hadn't they seen the stone thrower?

"Will someone please call the police?" Nancy's father asked.

A man hurried off to a nearby street telephone while curious onlookers peered inside the car to look at the rock.

Finally one young man remarked, "That stone is big enough to kill a person. I'd say you're lucky nothing happened to you."

A boy said, "Good you had shatterproof glass and the window was shut. Guess you have air-conditioning, sir?"

Mr Drew nodded.

Within minutes a patrol car roared up with two officers in it. They quickly examined the hole in the window and the rock on the floor.

Finally one of them said, "Do you have any enemies?"

"No," Mr Drew, Nancy, and Ned replied in unison. They thought of the burglar but did not believe he would deliberately try to harm them.

The other officer said, "This could have been just malicious mischief. In any case, we'll try to find out who did it."

He locked the police car and the two officers, carrying flashlights, went down a driveway between two shops. They returned in a little while and reported that no one had been hiding in the area at the rear.

"It's going to be pretty hard finding the guilty person," one of the officers admitted. "But maybe someone in the neighbourhood will talk."

"Hope you have better luck than I did," Mr Drew said. He explained that none of the curious onlookers admitted witnessing the attack.

One of the officers said to Mr Drew, "Until we track down the culprit, it'll be dangerous for you folks to stick around this place. Don't you think you ought to go home?"

Reluctantly Nancy agreed, but on the way she asked Ned, "Could you stay at our house tonight and come back here with me tomorrow morning?"

"I guess I can work it out," Ned replied. "Some people I was trying to sell insurance to told me to come back tomorrow afternoon."

"I wish you luck," said Nancy. "More luck than I seem to have solving this mystery."

Mr Drew patted her shoulder. "Mysteries are usually solved more by hard work than good luck."

Ned laughed. "In that case Nancy should have this mystery wound up in short order."

At ten o'clock the next morning Mr Drew took his car to the repair shop to have the broken window replaced. At the same time Ned and Nancy drove off in his convertible to the area of River Heights where the people of Greek and Turkish descent lived.

"We have only one other address," Nancy remarked. "Alime Gursel."

They found her apartment easily. She was a young married woman with a baby girl of about six months old in her arms.

"She's not the girl who ran away from the burglar," Nancy told herslf. Aloud she said, "Good morning," and smiled. "We're not trying to sell anything. We're hoping to find a couple of people but don't have their addresses. They probably live around here and I wondered if perhaps you might know them."

"Do come in," the young woman said. "Isn't my baby girl sweet?"

"She's darling," Nancy replied.

"Yes, she's a nice baby," Ned agreed.

Mrs Gursel motioned for her guests to follow her to the living room and they all seated themselves. Nancy was about to question her, when Mrs Gursel got up and came towards Ned.

"You know her daddy is away a great deal. He travels. My poor baby doesn't have a father to cuddle her. Would you mind holding her for a few minutes and giving her a little fatherly love?"

At the look of fright on Ned's face Nancy almost went into gales of laughter. Before Ned could refuse, Mrs Gursel laid the baby in his arms. He held her awkwardly, apparently fearful he would drop her. Finally he set the baby on his knee with both arms around her.

"Oh, she likes you!" Alime Gursel exclaimed. "Do put her over your shoulder and hug her."

By this time Nancy was smiling broadly. Ned looked at her pathetically as if to say, "Please take this creature away."

Obediently the Emerson College football star carefully lifted the baby, put her head in his neck, and suddenly his expression changed.

"She is nice," he said.

Nancy, managing to keep a straight face, asked the child's mother if she knew Tunay Arik or Aisha Hatun.

Mrs Gursel repeated the names, then slowly shook

her head. "I'm sorry," she said, "I not only do not know them, but I have never heard of either of them. Probably they do not live in this neighbourhood."

Ned stood up. "Probably not. Nancy, we'd better go," he said, and quickly handed the baby back to her mother.

Nancy told Mrs Gursel she had enjoyed their little visit, and the couple left. When they reached the street, Nancy could contain herself no longer and began to laugh.

"Oh, Ned, I wish I could have taken a picture of you when Mrs Gursel handed over her baby."

Ned frowned. "It's a good thing you didn't. I would have torn it up."

Quickly he changed the subject. "Now what do you intend to do? You don't have a single lead on those two other people."

"No, I don't," Nancy said ruefully. "But I'm sure they live in this area because of what Mr Akurzal said in his note. Let's ask in various shops. At some time or other Tunay Arik and Aisha Hatun must have to buy food."

She and Ned visited a supermarket, a launderette, and a stationery store without learning anything.

"Maybe," Ned remarked, "they grow their own food, have washing machines, and make their own paper and pencils."

"Very funny," said Nancy. "Ned, will you be serious!" But she couldn't keep a straight face.

"Well, where else?" he asked.

"I can think of only one other kind of place," Nancy answered. "A sweetshop."

"I saw one down on the next corner," Ned told her.

The couple walked to it and went in. Ned bought a box of chocolates and handed it to Nancy.

"Oh, thank you," she said, then asked the clerk, "Do you have any customers named Arik and Hatun?"

As the clerk said no, Nancy and Ned became aware of giggling at the side of the shop. They turned to see two little girls sucking lollipops. On a hunch Nancy asked if they knew either of the people.

"Sue, you tell her," said the other girl shyly.

"Okay, Kathy," her playmate said. She told Nancy that a family who lived next door to her had a boarder named Arik. "He has a funny first name. We call him Tunafish."

The two little girls burst into giggles again.

Nancy smiled and said, "Sue and Kathy, is it Tunay?"

"Guess so," Kathy answered. "We like Tunafish."

Nancy asked, "Will you take us there?"

"Why not?" said Sue.

The two little girls ran from the shop with Nancy and Ned at their heels. They went round a corner and up to a row of houses.

Presently they stopped and Kathy pointed. "He lives in there."

Nancy and Ned climbed the steps and rang the bell. A women answered and this time Ned made the enquiry. "Does Tunay Arik live here?"

"Yes, he does," the woman replied. "But he's at work now. Won't be home till five o'clock. Why did you want him?"

"We have a message for a man we think is named Tunay Arik," Nancy spoke up. "What does your boarder look like?"

When the woman gave a description, Nancy merely said, "He sounds like the right man. We'll be back to see him later."

As she and Ned turned to go down the steps, Nancy whispered to him, "He fits the description of the burglar all right!"

When they reached the foot of the steps, Sue and Kathy were waiting for them. Giggling again, they began to sing in a kind of nursery rhyme.

> "Tunafish is in lu-uv,
> Tunafish is in lu-uv.
> But Aisha won't date him.
> No, she'll never date him."

Nancy was intrigued. She clapped and asked the little girls to sing the song again. They obliged and ended up laughing so hard tears came to their eyes.

Nancy asked, "Do you mean Aisha Hatun?"

The girls said they did not know her last name, but a couple of times they had heard Tunafish singing softly in some foreign language. The song always began, "Ah-ee-sha, Ah-ee-sha."

"What else did he do?" Nancy enquired.

Sue and Kathy, who said they were sisters, admitted sneaking into the house next door now and then to listen to the boarders.

"Sometimes," said Kathy, "Tunafish would go to the telephone and dial a numer. He would say, 'Aisha, I must meet you.' Then he'd talk in another language. We'd get tired of listening and go home."

Ned grinned. "So you never found out where the girl lives?"

"No," Kathy said. "And he was so sad. I guess she wouldn't date him."

The girls said they must be going now and ran up the steps into the next house.

"We picked up a clue," Nancy remarked, "but we still have to locate Aisha Hatun. I have a hunch. Let's try the library. I noticed one not far from here."

They walked to it and Nancy found that the woman at the desk was a music teacher whom she knew.

"Hello, Nancy," she said. "I guess you're surprised to see me here. Most of my pupils go away in the summer and I take this part-time job. How come you're in this neighbourhood? Sleuthing?"

Nancy admitted that she was and introduced Ned to Mrs Armstrong. She told of her search for Aisha Hatun.

Mrs Armstrong pulled out her card file and thumbed through.

"Here it is," she said. "Miss Aisha Hatun takes out books quite regularly. She must be a great reader. Oh, oh. She has two overdue books." After a moment's pause, Mrs Armstrong continued, "She lives at 26 Dawson Street."

Nancy was thrilled to have the address. At last she seemed to be getting somewhere on the mystery.

Mrs Armstrong went on, "She lives with a couple named Kosay."

Nancy thanked the librarian, said she was glad to see her again, and went off. It was only a few minutes' walk to 26 Dawson Street.

The Kosay house was small with attractive bushes and a wild profusion of gay-coloured flowers.

"Pretty garden," Nancy remarked.

As she and Ned walked up to the house, he said, "If this is the girl you're looking for, how will I know it?"

Nancy answered quickly, "If she's the one who opens the door, I'll gently step on your foot. If someone else comes and we have to go inside and you and I are separated when she comes into the room, I'll smooth my hair back."

Nancy's pulse quickened as she rang the bell. Half a minute later the door was opened by a very attractive young woman with long black hair. Nancy stepped on Ned's foot.

12

Faker Revealed

The girl standing in the doorway was the same one who had torn herself away from the burglar!

Nancy tried not to show her excitement and asked, "Are you Miss Aisha Hatun?"

"Yes. You are looking for me?"

At close range the young woman was even prettier than at a distance. But she had a very sad look. She apparently did not recognize Nancy and set her big eyes on Ned admiringly.

For the first time Nancy did not know how to begin a conversation. Aisha certainly did not look like a person who would be a friend of a burglar!

Ned saved Nancy the trouble of launching into the subject. "You are Greek, or perhaps Turkish?" he asked.

Aisha looked bewildered at her questioners but answered, "I came from Istanbul, but I have lived here with my aunt and uncle for several years."

"You have a very pretty accent," Ned complimented her. "Do you speak other languages besides Turkish and English?"

For the first time Aisha smiled a little. "I do speak

French and Greek," she answered, then added, "Please tell me who you are and what you want."

Ned introduced himself and explained that Nancy was an amateur detective.

"Detective?" Aisha repeated, her eyes widening in fear.

There was a slight pause and finally Nancy said, "We're trying to find something and thought you might help us. But first, tell me about a friend of yours. Two little girls who live next door told us where he lives. His name is Tunay Arik."

Aisha's expression changed. She no longer looked sad nor did she smile. With a frown she said scornfully, "He is not a friend." Then she added, "Will you come inside, please? I would like to talk with you."

Nancy and Ned followed the girl into the living room. It occurred to Nancy that this was like being transported suddenly into another country. The entire decor was Turkish. There was a beautiful hand-woven Oriental rug on the floor, carved furniture, and several brass filigree lamps with matching oval shades.

After Aisha and her callers had sat down, she said to Nancy, "I recognize you now. You are the girl who was coming after me with the police and Arik told me to run. But why?"

Nancy hedged. She said, "No reason at all," and smiled. "I don't look dangerous, do I?"

"Oh no."

Nancy asked, "Didn't Arik tell you why he wanted you to run away?"

"No."

Ned spoke up, saying he thought this was rather strange. "And he hasn't phoned you since?"

Aisha said her aunt had taken a call from him while the girl was out, but she had not returned it.

She suddenly set her jaw and said, "I don't like Tunay Arik. I never have liked him but he keeps bothering me to date him. I never will."

"But you did meet him on the street," Nancy reminded her.

"Yes, I admit it. He phoned that he had received a very important letter from Istanbul which I must read at once. He said that since I would not let him come here, would I please meet him on that corner where you saw us." Tears came into Aisha's eyes.

Nancy and Ned looked at each other, wondering just how to proceed with the interview. Ned decided to be straightforward about it.

He asked, "Did the letter say that Farouk Tahmasp was dead?"

At the question Aisha burst into tears, raising one arm to her face to hide her emotions from the visitors. She got up, turned her back, and continued to sob.

But finally she spoke, looking straight at Nancy and Ned. "But how do you know this?"

Nancy did not answer the question direct. She walked over to the distraught girl, "Aisha, my father is a lawyer. He and I suspect that the letter Arik showed you is a forgery!"

"I do not understand," Aisha said. "A forgery?"

Nancy nodded. "We think Arik wrote that letter himself right here in River Heights. The paper was made in the United States and it's most unlikely that kind is sold in Turkey."

Aisha, who had pulled a handkerchief from a pocket, dried her eyes. "Tell me more of what you think. Tunay said a Greek friend named Seli sent it."

Nancy walked back to her chair and sat down. "Aisha," she said slowly, "we think there's a good possibility that Farouk Tahmasp is still alive!"

The Turkish girl looked into space for a moment, then cried out, "How wonderful! Oh, you think this is true?"

Ned answered. "We all do."

Aisha's whole attitude changed. Colour came back into her face and she smiled happily.

"Where is Farouk now?"

"We think," said Nancy, "that he's in Istanbul."

"Istanbul!" Aisha exclaimed. "So that's where he went."

She stared out the window. When her gaze returned to the callers, the sad look had come back into her face.

"I will tell you the whole story," she said, and sat down. "Farouk and I were in love and very happy. Then suddenly he got into some kind of trouble about smuggling. He never explained it to me but insisted he was innocent. Finally he ran away. I had a letter from him mailed in Paris explaining that he had decided to move out one night. After that I never heard from him again."

"When was that?" Ned asked.

"About two years ago. For months I waited for

another letter but nothing came. I didn't try to trace him because I thought he had found someone else."

On a hunch Nancy said, "Was it at that time Arik began trying to be friendly with you?"

Aisha nodded and said he was very persistent. "He sent me many gifts and would hide nearby so that when I came from the house he would catch up and walk along the street with me. But I would never go anywhere with him."

The girl paused for several seconds before going on. Taking a deep breath, she said, "I may as well tell you more. That day you saw me reading the letter, Tunay said, 'Now that Farouk is dead, there is no reason for you not to marry me.'"

At once Nancy recalled that she was looking for Arik because he was the one who tried to burglarize the Drew home!

She said, "Aisha, I think there's a very good reason why you shouldn't marry Arik. For one thing, your friend Farouk was proved innocent. My father, who handled his case, would like very much to find him and tell him so."

Aisha suddenly clapped her hands. "That is thrilling! Oh, he just has to be alive!"

Nancy and Ned asssured her that they and Mr Drew would do all they could to prove this.

"Here is my name and address," Nancy said, taking a card from her purse. "Now please do the following. Don't talk to Arik. In the meantime we'll try to find out if that letter he showed you was definitely a fake."

Aisha took the card and glanced at it. "I'll call you if I hear anything," she promised.

She looked so weary that Nancy decided they had better not talk any more. After all, the Turkish girl had been under a great emotional strain.

Nancy rose and said they must go. She put an arm around Aisha as they walked to the door. Impulsively the Turkish girl kissed her.

"You are a wonderful person," Aisha said. Casting her big eyes on Ned, she added, "And you too. Nancy is lucky to have you for a friend."

Ned grinned. "I think so."

Nancy gave him a sideways look and laughed softly. He opened the front door and waited for her to step outside. Then he followed.

Before they had a chance to say goodbye to Aisha, she said, "Oh, wait a minute! I forgot. When you first came you said you were hunting for something and thought I might be able to help you."

"That's right," Nancy replied. "It's about the mannequin in Farouk's window. Do you know where she is?"

To the surprise of Nancy and Ned a look of utter fright came over Aisha's face. Instead of answering, she quickly said goodbye and shut the door.

13

Mistaken Identity?

Ned began to laugh. "I don't often have doors shut in my face," he said.

Nancy was puzzled. Why had Aisha looked frightened? Apparently she knew something about the mannequin which she did not dare reveal.

Had George's guess been right that something valuable – and perhaps illegal – had been hidden inside the figure? She reminded Ned of this.

He did not think that the incident of Aisha shutting the door on them had any important significance. "Maybe she decided we were getting too nosy," he said. "Or – and here's a whole new idea for you, Miss Detective – if Aisha knows Farouk loves the mannequin, maybe she's jealous!"

This remark made Nancy laugh. "Well, I suppose our next move is to find out from Arik if that note was a fake."

"Where do you plan to start?" Ned queried.

Nancy said she thought they should go back to Tunay's rooming house and ask the owner where he worked. She grinned at Ned. "Suppose you talk to the suspect. He may recognize me and run off again."

"Okay," he agreed.

They set off for Arik's street, wondering if the two little girls would be around and might give them any further information about him. But they were not in sight. Nancy rang the bell of the rooming house. The same pleasant woman came to the door and without hesitation told the couple they would find Arik at the Bedford Carpet Factory.

"I don't know the street name, but it's somewhere along the river."

"I know where it is," said Nancy. "It has nice grounds and it's opposite a park."

"That's right," the woman said. "I always fix a lunch for Arik. He says he eats it in the park."

Nancy thanked her and the couple went off. They were delighted with this latest information. Now it would be fairly easy to spot Arik!

Since it was nearing lunchtime, Ned drove directly to the factory. For a long area in front of it there were 'no parking' signs so he had to drive to the next side street to leave the car. He and Nancy walked back along a high iron picket fence to the main entrance.

Suddenly Nancy grabbed Ned's arm. "Look!" she exclaimed. "Up by the office door!"

Ned glanced in that direction just in time to see a man, who had run out of the office, whip a black kerchief from his face. In his other hand he was carrying a bulging money sack.

"I bet he robbed the place!" Nancy cried out. Nearby was a street telephone booth. "Ned, I'll call the police."

"And I'll try to stop that man!" he said.

Nancy had just closed herself inside the glass booth when Ned noticed a car coming at a swift pace up the street. It was probably a getaway car!

By this time the robber was almost at the entrance to the grounds. Ned turned quickly on to the path. The next second he grabbed the man in a crunching football tackle.

The fellow went down and the money sack flew from his hand. Instantly Ned dashed to pick up the sack and threw it as far and hard as he could towards the office door.

In that split second the man rushed to the side walk and jumped into the car which had stopped. Ned was tempted to follow, but realized that both the robber and the driver might be armed. He did manage, however, to get the license number.

Before the car was out of sight, four policemen roared up in a sedan. Nancy dashed over to them and told what had happened, while Ned gave the license number. In a flash two of the officers took off after the robbers' car. The other two started up the walk towards the factory.

Ned looked at his companion. "This is one time the police must take over."

Nancy and Ned followed them, however. Ned pointed to the money sack and one of the officers picked it up. They all walked inside.

"Oh!" Nancy gasped.

On the floor near a desk lay a girl not much older than herself. She was unconscious but beginning to stir. One of the officers pulled a small vial of ammonia salts from his pocket and waved it under the girl's nostrils.

As her eyelids fluttered open, a door at the rear of the office opened and a heavy-set balding man entered. He looked in astonishment at the scene before him.

"What's going on?" he asked.

The officer holding the bag of money raised it. "Is this yours?" he asked.

"My payroll!" the man shouted. "What happened? Where did you get this?"

The officer responded, "This couple here can give you more details than I can."

As the young woman on the floor was helped to her feet and seated in a chair, Nancy and Ned told of coming along just in time to see the robber. They were reluctant to give details of their own part in the recovery of the payroll, but the policemen insisted upon a full report. The balding man who said he was Mr Bedford, the factory owner, thanked them profusely.

By this time his secretary was able to tell her part of the story. The bookkeeper had already gone out to lunch and she was in the office alone.

"A man came in wearing a black kerchief across his face. He pointed a gun at me and told me to lie down on the floor and not to make a sound. I was so scared I fainted."

"What did the fellow look like?" the policeman asked.

The girl said he had blond hair but that's all she could tell about him. Nancy and Ned gave a description. He was a medium height and clean-shaven.

Out of the corner of her eye, Nancy noticed the workers coming from a side door. If she and Ned were to find Arik, they should leave at once.

"I think we've given you all the information we can," Nancy said. "Now if you'll please excuse us – "

"I will be in touch with you," said Mr Bedford. "You have saved me thousands of dollars."

Nancy and Ned said goodbye and walked out of the door. They hurried down the walk and crossed over to the park. Nancy half hid behind a tree and watched the oncoming workers. A few minutes later she saw Tunay Arik.

"There he is!" she whispered to Ned.

The young man walked on past the other workers and chose an empty bench at the far side of the park. As he opened his lunch box and took out a sandwich, Ned sidled on to the bench beside him. Nancy, partly covering her face with one hand, sat down next to Ned. She leaned back slightly, half hiding herself.

Presently Ned said, "Excuse me, but aren't you Tunay Arik?"

The young man gave a start and rose from the bench. Ned pulled him back. "Don't try to run away again. I want answers to three questions. First, that letter you showed Aisha was a forgery, wasn't it?"

Arik looked frightened and did not answer.

Ned went on, "Farouk Tahmasp is alive, isn't he?"

Finally Arik, like someone trapped, said, "Why –

why yes, but that is a personal matter. I meant no harm by getting someone to write that letter for me."

Ned looked at Arik in disgust. He now said, "Why did you try to steal the Turkish rug from the Drew home?"

Arik turned ash white. Now he tried once more to get up. Ned yanked him back.

"Answer me!" he said severely.

"I'm not bad! I'm not a burglar!" Arik said in a hoarse whisper. "I didn't try to steal anything. Say, who are you, anyway? A cop?"

"No, I'm not a policeman," Ned replied.

Arik had eaten nothing. Now he closed his lunch box and insisted he must get back to work. "I haven't done anything wrong," he insisted.

Nancy spoke up. She was not convinced that he was telling the truth. Trying to take him by surprise, she said, "Where did you get the super-duper master key that opened the kitchen door to our house?"

Arik looked totally blank. "I don't know what you're talking about," he replied.

The girl detective went on, "I see you don't wear your fancy gold filigree bracelet to work."

Arik stood up, his eyes flashing angrily. "I don't own a bracelet and I think you two are crazy. Now don't try to stop me again or you will be in trouble."

Nancy looked the man straight in the eyes. "If it wasn't you who came to my house, then you have a double. Do you know who he is?"

"No." Arik strode across the park and went straight back to the factory.

After he had gone, Nancy and Ned began to discuss whether or not he was guilty.

"He certainly acted innocent enough," Ned remarked.

Nancy said she was beginning to doubt herself. "After all, the first time I saw him, when he was trying to steal the rug, it was only by lamplight. I could be mistaken."

"Anything's possible," Ned said, "but on second thoughts that guy admitted knowing Farouk." He frowned, adding, "Nothing makes sense."

Nancy did not reply. She had another hunch and decided to telephone her father at once and tell him what had happened. She crossed the street and once more closed herself in the telephone booth and gave him a full report. Mr Drew said he was glad she had called him. He would have a tail put on Arik at once.

"And I'll keep my eyes open for a double," Nancy told him.

When she rejoined Ned, he declared he was starving. "Want to go back to that Greek restaurant?" he teased.

Nancy laughed. "I guess we'd better not. How about a nice unmysterious café?"

As soon as they had finished eating, Ned glanced at his watch to see how much time he had left before his appointment.

"I can spend exactly one more hour with you," he said. "Where would you like to go?"

"Home," Nancy replied promptly. "I haven't worked on the Turkish rug for some time. Let's see if we can find more words in the border. I still think there are further directions in it."

"Okay," said Ned.

When they reached the Drew house, Hannah Gruen was not there and Nancy was surprised to find the Turkish rug rolled up on the floor of the front hall. Why was it there? Surely Mrs Gruen would not have brought it downstairs since she felt so strongly that it should be kept hidden in Nancy's cupboard.

As Ned closed the front door and turned towards her, Nancy picked up the rug and began to unroll it quickly. The next moment a small scimitar flew from the inside and headed straight for Ned!

14

Well-Kept Secret

Quick as a flash Ned sidestepped the flying scimitar which missed him by an inch. It embedded itself in the wall near the front door.

"Wow!" he cried out. "What's going on here? Some welcome!"

"Thank goodness you're all right," said Nancy. "I wish I knew what's going on."

At that moment they heard a key turn in the front-door lock and they both stiffened. Was the burglar returning?

Ned got ready to jump him and Nancy moved away. To their relief the door was opened by Hannah Gruen. She looked in surprise at the positions of Nancy and Ned. Then she spotted the scimitar protruding from the wall.

"Oh my goodness!" she said. "Where did that thing come from?"

"It was rolled up in the rug," Nancy replied. "Hannah, did you by any chance bring the rug down here?"

"No, I didn't. I thought we had agreed to hide it in your cupboard."

"We did," Nancy said, "so apparently the burglar brought it down. But how did he know where we had hidden the rug?"

Hannah interposed, "And assuming it was the same intruder, why didn't he take the rug when he had the chance?"

"Can't answer either of your questions," Ned replied. "But one thing's sure – "

"Arik isn't our man," Nancy finished Ned's sentence.

Briefly they explained to Hannah that Arik was at work when the intruder came to the Drew house.

As Hannah started to take the scimitar from the wall, Nancy suggested that they did not touch it. "It may have fingerprints useful to the police," she said.

Ned chuckled. "You sure have been contacting the police lately," he teased, and told how he and Nancy had captured the robber down at the Bedford Carpet Factory.

Hannah was astouned but shook her head resignedly. "Ned," she said, "you should have learned by this time that adventure comes Nancy's way even when she's not looking for it."

"That's one reason it's so interesting to be with her," he replied.

Nancy and Hannah made a search of the house but found nothing missing. The young detective headed for the phone to call her friend Chief McGinnis. The two discussed the whole case for some time. He told her to leave the scimitar where it was until a couple of his men could pick it up.

"They are pretty busy right now," he said. "It will probably be near suppertime before anyone comes."

Meanwhile Ned and Hannah had started to examine the rug to see if it had been damaged. Fortunately it had not been.

When Nancy joined them, he said, "Maybe it's an old Turkish custom to leave a scimitar as a warning."

Mrs Gruen looked worried and remarked, "It gives me the creeps to think that somebody can get into this house despite all our excellent locks."

The three went all round the place, checking windows and doors and finally concluded that the burglar had come in through the front door on his second trip.

Suddenly Nancy looked round and said, "Hannah, where's Togo?"

"I took him to the Dog Beauty Parlor," the housekeeper said. She glanced at her watch and added, "It's about time to pick up our little dog."

"I'd do it," Ned said, "but I must leave now to keep my appointment."

"Thanks, Ned, for coming along today," Nancy said.

"You know I don't mind," he replied. "I'll let you know if I make my sale."

Nancy wished him luck, then drove into town to get the dog. He frisked about, not only glad to see her, but acting as if he were proud of his new appearance. He had been pedicured, shampooed and his coat brushed until it shone.

"You're beautiful!" Nancy said, scooping Togo up in her arms.

She carried him to the car and drove home. No sooner had Togo bounded into the living room than he spied the scimitar in the wall. He growled at it loudly, then jumped up and knocked it down.

"Oh!" Nancy cried out. "Get away! You'll cut yourself!"

She picked up the scimitar and laid it on top of the piano. Then Nancy realized what she had done. Her own fingerprints might have blotted out those the burglar had left!

"Oh, Togo, sometimes you're good and sometimes you cause a lot of trouble!"

The terrier merely looked at Nancy and wagged his tail.

"You're hopeless!"she told the dog.

The telephone rang and Nancy went into the hall to answer it. To her amazement and delight Aisha was calling.

"Nancy, will you ever forgive me?" the girl said. "I was so rude to you this morning. I am extremely sorry."

"Of course," Nancy replied. "I assumed you knew some secret in connection with the mannequin that you didn't want to tell me."

"That is true," said Aisha. "But I do want to talk to you. I am alone. My aunt and uncle just went out and will be gone for a while. Could you and your friend come?"

Nancy said that Ned had already left but she would be glad to drive over. She told Hannah where she was going and went out of the door, her mind in a whirl.

What was the Turkish girl going to tell her? Did she know the whereabouts of the mannequin? Would she reveal more about Farouk? Nancy finally reached Aisha's street, parked her convertible, and went up the walk to the porch steps.

The Turkish girl opened the door before Nancy had a chance to ring. Impulsively she put an arm round Nancy as they walked into the living room.

The girls sat down and Aisha began her story. "As I told you, I know where Farouk's mannequin is. But you'll never find her unless Farouk himself tells you where she is."

"Why not?" Nancy asked, bewildered. She wondered why Farouk would have asked her father to bring the mannequin to Turkey if he would not reveal where she was.

Aisha said that he had made her promise she would not reveal the secret.

"I can't understand why," Nancy told her quite frankly. "By keeping it a secret, it sounds as if there is something dishonest about the whole thing."

Aisha looked a little frightened to hear this. "I assure you there was nothing dishonest about the mannequin or about Farouk wanting to keep her whereabouts a secret." She changed the subject. "Nancy, tell me why you want to find the mannequin."

"I suppose I've been as mysterious about this whole thing as you," the young detective replied, laughing.

Nancy divulged the story of the rug, all the time watching Aisha's face closely. The girl's expression kept changing from one of happiness to one of puzzlement. She made no comment even when Nancy finished.

"Would you like to see the rug?" the young detective asked her.

"Very much."

"Then let's go over to my house. Perhaps you can find more words or symbols in it that will reveal the entire message."

As soon as they reached the house Nancy introduced Aisha to Hannah. Then the two girls sat down to study the rug. Aisha was intrigued by all that Nancy and her friends had found so far.

Industriously they continued to examine the border. Minutes went by, then the Turkish girl exclaimed that she had found something. She pointed it out to Nancy.

"Look there among the leaves!" Aisha exclaimed.

Woven in among them was a fancy and unusual-looking object.

"It's a shoeshine stand," Aisha explained.

"I've never seen one like it," Nancy remarked.

"They are fairly common in Istanbul," the Turkish girl went on. "I cannot figure out why Farouk added this to the border. Nancy, can you guess?"

"Not right now. Surely a rug dealer wouldn't be shining shoes!" she declared. "But there's another angle I must investigate."

In reply to Aisha's puzzled frown, Nancy added that when it was possible she would try to trace Farouk through rug shops in Istanbul.

"Oh, you're marvellous!" her friend exclaimed.

"Maybe there's another symbol that will be more of a clue," Nancy said.

The two girls searched diligently but found nothing more. They decided to rest and have a cool drink. While sipping cherry soda, Nancy told her visitior about the burglar's intrusions and the scimitar and showed it to her.

The Turkish girl shivered a little. "That is horrible!" she cried out.

"One thing is certain," Nancy said. "Arik didn't leave it, and if the man who did is the one who was here before, then Arik is innocent. I was sure I had identified him as the burglar – I didn't want to tell you this before – but during the time someone sneaked in here today he was at work and talking with Ned and me.

"The burglar that we suspect," Nancy went on, "is a man who looks very much like Arik, is a super-duper locksmith, and wears a gold filigree bracelent with turquoise in it."

Aisha said she knew no one like that and now she must leave. "I'll take the bus home," she said. "I want to stop off and do a little shopping. Nancy, I am so glad to be friends with you and truly I wish I could tell you where the mannequin is, but I cannot break a promise until I receive permission."

"I understand," said Nancy.

Aisha had been gone only a few minutes when two policemen arrived. Nancy showed them the scimitar and said they would find her fingerprints on it as well as those of the intruder.

One of the officers remarked, "This is a cheap, handmade scimitar. But that might make it easier to find the person who left it than if it were an imported expensive one."

He took a cloth bag from his pocket and slipped the scimitar into it. Then he and his companion went off.

Nancy, her mind full of many things, began to open her mail, which had been delivered earlier in the day. To her delight the travel brochure which Mr Simpson had promised to send was among her letters. She glanced at the itinerary excitedly, then curled up in a living-room chair to open the rest of the mail. There was nothing interesting and she fell to daydreaming about the mystery.

The front doorbell rang twice but Nancy did not seem to hear it. Hannah answered and accepted two packages from the deliverymen. The bell rang a third time and once more Mrs Gruen came into the front hall. She glanced into the living room and looked at Nancy, thinking that perhaps she had fallen asleep. But the young detective was staring up at the ceiling and counting on her fingers. Hannah shook her head and went on.

She opened the front door and Bess and George came in. Seeing their friend in the living room, they walked in. Nancy came out of her reverie.

"Hi!" she said, uncurling herself. "Oh, girls, I've been working and working on the mystery and now I think I've solved part of it!"

"You have!" the cousins said.

Nancy smiled and looked directly at the two of them. "Yes, but I'll have to go to Istanbul to prove it. Could you two go with me?"

·15·

Travel Plans

Nancy's announcement about the trip to Turkey came as a complete surprise. Bess and George stared at her, speechless.

Nancy grinned at them. "I mean it. And it would be great if Ned and Burt and Dave could go too. And also Aisha. I have the itinerary."

George was the first to recover from her surprise. She exclaimed, "Don't tell me you've found the mannequin!"

"No, but I did learn this. There's a big secret connected with the mannequin. Aisha knows where she is. But she says Farouk made her promise not to tell it."

Bess frowned. "I'm all mixed up over this whole thing. Please somebody straighten me out. *Please!*"

"I have decided," said Nancy, "that since we're sure Farouk sent the rug and he's in Istanbul and he has been declared innocent of the smuggling charge, and he and Aisha were in love, what we have to do now is to help the two of them get together."

"But after we all get to Istanbul how are we going to find Farouk? It's a big city. Just walk the streets until he shows up?" George remarked.

Nancy revealed the latest clue in the border of the rug. "It's a special, highly decorated shoeshine stand. I believe Farouk expects Dad to show up near one of them."

"I can imagine how many there must be." Bess sighed, then asked, "Do you suppose Farouk will be awfully disappointed if you don't bring the mannequin along?"

Nancy shrugged and George remarked, "If he's not planning to come back to America, and wants the mannequin badly enough, he can tell us where it is and we'll ship it to him."

Bess and George were enthusiastic about the idea of going to Turkey. "Where's the itinerary you mentioned?"

Nancy picked it up from the table near the wing chair, and handed it to the cousins.

"Hypers!" George exclaimed as she gazed at the colourful pictures of mosques and caiques.

Bess said, "George, let's phone our parents right now for permission!"

"Wait!" Nancy cried as Bess started towards the phone.

She had heard her father's car pulling into the driveway. As soon as the lawyer had greeted everyone, she put her proposal to him.

He looked startled, but after thinking over the matter, remarked, "It sounds like a good idea. But what about the expense? Where would all you young people find the travel money?"

Nancy reminded her father about Mr Simpson, the

travel agent. "You recall he had arranged an inexpensive trip for a group to Turkey. Perhaps we could take advantage of the low plane fare without going on the rest of his tour."

As she spoke, Nancy indicated the round-trip fare at the bottom of the brochure. "We could stay in Istanbul and search for Farouk."

"Well," said Mr Drew, "phone Mr Simpson and see if he has eight reservations left. But don't get your hopes too high."

Nancy invited Bess and George to stay to dinner, then hurried of to make the call. The travel agency's line was busy. She sat waiting, tapping her fingers on the telephone table. She tried again. Still no luck.

"Somebody must be arranging a trip around the world," she thought.

This time she waited a little longer and was successful in reaching him.

"Nancy Drew, how are you?" he asked. "All the Simpsons are fine, including little Tommy. He calls you his water wheel lady."

Nancy chuckled. "I'm glad he hasn't forgotten me. Mr Simpson, thank you for the itinerary of your tour to Turkey. By any chance, do you have eight places left? If so, could my dad and I and six friends just make the trip to and from Itanbul without taking the whole tour of Turkey?"

"Let me take a look," Mr Simpson replied.

He left the phone to consult his chart, but soon returned. "I have good news for you, Nancy," he said. "Two people have just cancelled and that makes exactly eight seats available. You know, of course, we leave in two days. Do you have passports and vaccinations?"

"Yes," Nancy replied. "I haven't asked all my friends yet, but I'm sure they'll be able to make it. May I let you know tomorrow?"

"That will be fine."

When Nancy came back into the living room with the good news, Bess and George each gave a "yae" and Bess hurried to call her parents. She returned in a moment, saying she had their consent to make the trip. Then George phoned the Fayne house and received her parents' permission.

At that moment Hannah Gruen came into the living room and was told about the exciting plan. "I'm glad," she said. "Now Nancy and Mr Drew can get away from people who break into houses and leave scimitars and throw rocks at cars."

"And don't worry, Hannah," put in Mr Drew, "I'll see that Chief McGinnis sends a patrol car out here regularly to make sure everything stays peaceful while we're away."

"Now that's not necessary," she said, then went on, "I came to tell you that dinner is ready. And since we're having steak, you'd better come to the table at once."

Mr Drew chuckled. "I'll be with you in a jiffy." He hurried off but was back in three minutes. Then they all went to the dining room.

As soon as dinner was over, Nancy went to the telephone. The first one she called was Aisha. When

Nancy mentioned the trip, the Turkish girl gave a little cry of happiness. Then she said she was not quite sure.

"I'm thrilled, but I am a little fearful of meeting Farouk."

"Once you see each other, I'm sure everything will be wonderful," said Nancy. "Aisha, could you go for a drive with me tomorrow morning? There are several things I'd like to discuss with you. One of them concerns arrangements for us to stay in places that would not be expensive."

"I'm sure my parents can find something," Aisha replied. "And I'll be very happy to meet you tomorrow morning. What time?"

"Ten o'clock. By then I should know how many of us can go."

Sure that Ned would say yes, she put in a call to his home. She hoped he had made the insurance sale that afternoon. It would help pay for the trip!

Ned answered. "Hello."

"Hi!" said Nancy. "Ned, do you still want to be my bodyguard?"

"Nancy. You mean in Istanbul?"

"Yes. Could you go in two days?"

"Wow! Let me get my breath. You mean it?"

Upon hearing it was a bona fide trip, he laughed. "You bet I'll go. Wouldn't miss it for anything. I sold a big enough policy today to pay all my expenses."

"Good for you," said Nancy.

Bess was the next one to come to the phone and

tried several places to find Dave. She finally left word at his home for him to call at Nancy's.

George had no better luck locating Burt. It was not until the following morning that both boys phoned Nancy's house and heard of the exciting trip. Shortly before ten o'clock they called back to say they would be able to accompany the group.

"Sounds cool," said Dave. "I think I'll pretend to be a sultan and you girls are some of my slaves!"

Nancy laughed and replied, "You just try it and I'll cover your whole head with my Turkish veil!"

Quickly Nancy dialled Mr Simpson's travel agency to confirm the number of plane reservations, then she hurried off in her car to meet Aisha. The two girls spent a very pleasant hour together, and Aisha said she would arrange for the whole group to have good accomodations in Istanbul. "I will cable my parents as soon as I get home." As the Turkish girl was about to step out of the convertible she impulsively gave Nancy a tight squeeze. "You're the most wonderful detective in the world," she said. Nancy smiled and kissed her new friend, then she drove off.

"I think I'll stop at Mr Anthony's tailor shop and see if Haw-Haw is there. Maybe I can get him to answer a few questions. I'm sure that funny old fellow knows more than he's telling!"

Fortunately he was there, perched as usual on a bench in the corner of the shop. As soon as he saw Nancy, Haw-Haw began to laugh on a crescendo note that resembled a shriek. It sent chills up and down the girl's spine.

Finally he stopped laughing and said, "You keep coming back here, miss. You think that mannequin's a-hidin' somewhere around this place?"

"Maybe. If you see her, let me know," Nancy replied. Then she walked over to the man and looked straight at him. On a sudden hunch she asked, "What I want to know is, who is the man you're giving information to about me?"

For once Haw-Haw did not laugh. His eyes shifted nervously. The young detective was sure that she had hit upon the truth!

Finally he said, "How'd you find out? I didn't think it would hurt."

Nancy was thrilled that he had fallen into her trap! Still looking stern, she said, "It matters a great deal. Now tell me, who is he?"

The wizened old man wilted. He looked all around, then whispered, "He's a cousin of Tunay Arik. Pretty near his double, I'd say. He's from Istybull."

Haw-Haw's lighter side returned. He gave a low chuckle. "All this time you thought Tunay Arik was the burglar when really it was his cousin."

"They've got an interesting grapevine," Nancy said to herself. "Tunay told his cousin about our encounter at the carpet factory. The cousin in turn told Haw-Haw."

Realizing the old man knew even more than she had suspected, Nancy asked him why Arik's cousin wanted the rug.

"He found out Farouk sent the rug to your father and thought that valuable jewels were sewn into it.

He went right over to your house and tried to steal it."

Nancy was elated with the information. She said, "When the burglar found out there weren't any jewels in the rug, he became furious. He left me a scimitar as a souvenir. Do you know why?"

Haw-Haw's jaw sagged and his eyes bulged. He was the very picture of a terrified man. Finally he spoke, "I'll show you something," he said.

He put one hand inside his coat. Suddenly it occurred to Nancy that he might be reaching for a weapon!

Important Confession

Haw-Haw pulled a scimitar from his inside coat pocket. Before he might have a chance to use it, Nancy grabbed his arm and yanked it upward.

"Ga-ga-ga – " the man gurgled.

The scimitar fell to the floor. Then, to Nancy's horror, Haw-Haw collapsed.

"What you do?" the tailor cried, getting up from his chair and rushing over.

Nancy tried to explain that she was afraid Haw-Haw was going to stab her, but Mr Anthony did not seem to understand. By this time Nancy had laid Haw-Haw flat on his back.

Nancy tried to resuscitate him but realized that the victim probably needed oxygen.

"Do you have a phone?" she asked the tailor.

"No."

"I'll be back," Nancy said. "Do not move him."

Alarmed, she raced to a street telephone booth and called for the police ambulance. It arrived quickly. A doctor and an officer hurried into the tailor's shop. Nancy recognized the latter as one of the two policemen who were going to hunt down the person that had thrown the stone at her father's car.

After a quick examination the doctor called for a pulmotor. As the officer administered oxygen, the physician gave the old man a heart massage.

While the men were working, Nancy picked up the scimitar. It was a duplicate of the one which had nearly injured Ned!

All this while the little tailor had been pacing back and forth, wringing his hands and evidently praying. He stopped when he saw Nancy gazing at the scimitar. He looked at it too.

"His?" he asked, pointing towards Haw-Haw.

"I think not," Nancy replied. "There is a name on here. It is Aslanapa."

The tailor shook his head. "I not know him."

Nancy decided that whoever had planted the scimitar in the prayer rug had made sure there was no mark of identification on the weapon. She wondered if Aslanapa was the name of the maker or possibly of the burglar. She would just have to wait until Haw-Haw revived and ask him.

When he did regain consciousness, the old man was too weak to talk. The physician ordered that he be taken to he hospital at once, so Nancy had no chance to question him.

While Haw-Haw was being placed in the ambulance, the officer turned to Nancy. "Miss Drew, we meet again. I'm sorry I haven't any news for you. We didn't find any witnesses to the rock incident, much less suspects."

Nancy had assumed as much. She showed the officer the scimitar and pointed out the name on it.

She then explained it had been in Mr Hyde's possession.

"It's a duplicate of the one which was left at my house by an unknown intruder," she said.

"Chief McGinnis has every man on the alert. We'll get him!" the officer assured her.

He made some notes in his report book, then the ambulance went off, its siren shrieking. Nancy went home, thinking this certainly had been an eventful day. She hoped Haw-Haw would be all right.

Nancy found Hannah getting Mr Drew's clothes ready for the trip. She told her what had happened.

The housekeeper looked concerned, but then smiled. "I presume you'll keep on having adventures up till the moment you get on the plane. I suggest that you start thinking about your own wardrobe. Are you going to pack the rug too?"

Nancy shook her head. "No. It will take up too much room."

Nancy was just entering her bedroom when the telephone rang. She answered it in her father's study. The hospital was calling and had a message for her from Mr Hyde.

"He's much better," the nurse reported, "and the doctor said he might have visitors. Mr Hyde insists he must see you at once. He has something very important to tell you."

"I'll be right down," Nancy replied.

The hopsital had put Mr Hyde in a room with three other men. The old man motioned her to come close to his side.

"What I got to say to you is private," he whispered. "I wanted you to know you weren't to blame for what happened to me. I often get these heart spells."

"I'm sorry about that," Nancy murmured.

Haw-Haw went on, "Mostly I wanted you to know I wasn't going to hurt you. When you mentioned the scimitar I just wanted to show you the one I had."

"Where did you get it?"

Mr Hyde said it belonged to a man named Aslanapa. "I call him Nappy for short. He left it with me to sell."

"Where is he?" Nancy asked quickly.

"Nappy is the cousin to Arik I told you about, but Arik don't pay him no mind. He don't like him or trust him."

"Why?" Nancy's mind teemed with questions. If it was true that Tunay and his cousin did not get along, then why hadn't Arik admitted he had a double? Why hadn't he told her about his evil cousin? Was Arik afraid of his cousin, or perhaps involved in the scheme after all?

Haw-Haw said he did not know why Arik distrusted his cousin. Nappy seemed all right to him. "He makes master keys and scimitars. Pays me a good commission for selling them."

Haw-Haw heaved a great sigh. "I guess it ain't right at that and I want to tell you I ain't goin' to do it no more."

"If it's not legitimate, I'm glad to hear you're giving it up," said Nancy. "Tell me, where does Aslanapa live?"

"I don't know, and that's honest," said the wizened Mr Hyde.

"Then," Nancy told him, "he carried on his business with you away from his house?"

"That's right. We made all the exchanges in the tailor's shop. Fortunately Tony don't understand English much so we could say anything we wanted to and he never suspected anything."

Nancy asked him how he got the names of people who wanted to buy master keys. Haw-Haw took a long time before answering.

"I got quite a few friends in the underworld," he finally answered. "I expect they'll be mighty upset when they find out I'm not goin' to deal in those fancy keys no more."

Nancy thought, "And a lot of other people, including the police, will be glad to know it."

Haw-Haw went on to say that Nancy was probably wondering why he was telling her all this. The reason was that he had had a good scare a while ago and it had taught him a lesson."

"I could've died," he said, "and I'd hate to have what I've been telling you on my mind. I might even tell the police," he finished.

Nancy could see that the old man was getting tired, but before she had to leave him, she wanted to find out the answer to one more question.

"Mr Hyde, once when I asked you about the mannequin in Farouk Tahmasp's window you laughed at me."

"Yep, I did, but I wasn't laughin' at you. I was

recollectin' about Farouk and that wax figure – or whatever it was – of a girl he had in his window. The way he used to treat her! I could almost believe he was in love with that dummy!"

"What made you think so?" Nancy asked, surprised.

Haw-Haw grinned. "Why, you know, sometimes when he thought nobody on the street was lookin' he'd reach in the window and pat that thing and stroke her head. Once I even saw him kiss her cheek."

Nancy burst into laughter. Then she became serious again. "Have you any idea where Farouk put the mannequin when he left?"

Haw-Haw looked surprise. "You think he left her behind? No sirree. He thought too much of that Turkish mannequin. I'm sure he took her along."

Just then a nurse came in and said that the visiting period was up. Nancy said goodbye to the old man and wished him a speedy recovery.

Her next stop was River Heights Police Headquarters.

"Why, Nancy, what a pleasant surprise!" Chief McGinnis greeted her.

Briefly she related what Haw-Haw Hyde had told her regarding the burglar and scimitar incident at her house.

"I'm afraid I was a bit hasty thinking Mr Hyde would harm me," she added.

"Can't be too careful in your kind of work," the chief replied.

When she reached home Nancy went to her bedroom at once to do some packing. Hannah was already there. "I thought I'd give you some help," she said.

The housekeeper listened in amazement to the story of Haw-Haw's confession. All the time Nancy was talking she was pulling articles for the trip from her drawers. Suddenly Togo began to bark wildly in the front hall.

"Somebody must be on the porch," said Hannah, "but I didn't hear the bell ring."

"Maybe the bell is out of order," Nancy suggested. "I'll go down and see who it is."

As she reached the foot of the steps, Togo was jumping up against the door, whining and barking frantically.

Nancy opened the front door. At once Togo dashed outside and sprang at a huge Belgian shepherd dog.

"Oh, Togo will be torn to bits!" Nancy thought desperately and rushed out.

To her utter astonishment the big dog snarled at Togo but did not attack him. Instead he glared balefully at Nancy, then jumped on the girl and knocked her down. She tried to get up but he bowled her over again. This time she landed face down. He planted his huge front paws on her back and with all his weight held her there.

In vain Nancy tried to rise but the muscular animal was too strong for her. Now he began to growl. Any moment he might sink his teeth into her!

"Help!" Nancy cried out.

·17·

"Yok! Yok!"

Hannah Gruen looked out the window. She was horrified by the sight below her.

"Oh, Nancy!" she wailed.

The housekeeper hurried down the front stairs as fast as she could and raced out of the front door. As she approached the Belgian shepherd he growled menacingly, while still pinning Nancy to the ground.

Suddenly courage returned to Hannah Gruen. She rushed round the corner of the house to where a hose was coiled round a hook in the foundation. After quickly unwinding it, she turned on the water full force, then hurried to the front.

"Sorry to get you wet, Nancy," she called. "But I hope this will drive the beast away."

The dog did not like the water and kept twisting his head to avoid it. As Hannah approached him and the stream became more forceful, he suddenly shifted his position. His paws slipped from Nancy's back. She was free!

Keeping her back to Hannah, Nancy stepped out of the dog's way until she had reached the housekeeper's side. The animal, almost blinded by the hard stream of water, gradually turned away, whimpering and growling alternately. Finally he gave up and dripping wet slunk down the street.

Togo had escaped long before this and had hidden behind a large rhododendron bush. Now he reappeared, ran towards the sidewalk, and barked importantly as if he had been responsible for outwitting the big Belgian shepherd.

Hannah looked at Nancy. "You're certainly a sight. How do you feel?"

Nancy replied, "I feel like following that dog to his house. But I don't have to. I know whom he belongs to. I saw the name on his collar just before he knocked me down."

"Who owns such a fierce beast?"

"Aslanapa."

Hannah looked alarmed. "The man with the scimitars?"

The young detective nodded. "Hannah, it seems as if we are calling the police morning, noon, and night. But would you mind reporting that dog and the name on his collar?"

The housekeeper did this while Nancy went to take a shower. When she came downstairs, Mrs Gruen told her that the police had already captured the dog.

"They think he was set on you on purpose," she reported. "They traced the dog through its license tag and picked him up at the house where Aslanapa had been living. The police learned that he had told the boarding-house owner he was leaving, but did not say where he was going. Aslanapa had packed his clothes, taken the dog along, and said goodbye.

"The police said this was not unusual, because lodgers come and go frequently."

Nancy's brow furrowed in anger. "That man is a heartless crook!" she cried. "He apparently abandoned the dog."

"It's a good thing," Hannah replied. "The police said that the dog is a killer – that he had been army-trained. It was fortunate he didn't bite you. Perhaps he smelled Togo's scent on you and thought that you weren't unfriendly. He's at the pound in solitary confinement."

Nancy realized how lucky she had been. The dog might have killed her. She put the frightening incident out of her mind and said, "I wonder if Aslanapa, when he realized the rug did not contain valuable jewels, decided to go back to Turkey."

The Drews reported this possibility to the police who said they would stop the man if he tried to leave the country. They were sure that he intended to sneak out, probably under an assumed name.

Nancy finished her packing, then checked with her friends and with the travel bureau. Everything seemed to be running smoothly. Mr Drew and the four girls from River Heights were to meet the boys in New York the following afternoon. From there they would fly to Brussels, Belgium, then go directly to Istanbul.

That evening Nancy got in touch with Chief McGinnis, but he had no leads on the vanished Aslanapa. The next day when Nancy told the full story to the group at the New York airport, all of them were sure her path and Aslanapa's would cross in Istanbul.

"I hope he won't set another ferocious dog on you!" Bess said.

The wait in Brussels was short and the travellers reached the Istanbul airport a few hours later. Sunday had literally flown by and according to Turkish time it was near noon on Monday.

Ned spoke up, "Our group is so large, I guess we'll have to go in two *dolmus*." He grinned at the others. "That means taxi."

The tour leader, Mr Randolph, wished them all a pleasant stay in Istanbul. "Now you're on your own."

All this time Aisha had been looking round for her parents. Suddenly she saw them. The others smiled as the couple clasped her in their arms. Then she introduced Mr and Mrs Hatun. Aisha looked just like her pretty mother.

The family lived in western Turkey, but had arranged for rooms at the homes of two friends with large houses. The girls would stay at one, Mr Drew and the boys at the other.

"My parents will spend a short time here," Aisha said. "When you leave, I will go and make them a long visit."

After their luggage was assembled, two *dolmus* were summoned. Mrs Hatun invited the girls to ride with her and her daughter. Since the mother spoke little English, Aisha became their guide.

Mr Drew and the boys joined Mr Hatun in the

other taxi. Their driver, who spoke fluent English, introduced himself as a student at the University of Istanbul. Once they were on their way, he did not have to be prompted to identify the famous landmarks.

The airport was out of town, but as they approached the city, both guides pointed out a mammoth circular wall. "That encompassed the old city," Aisha told the girls.

Soon they came to a bridge which was named after Ataturk, Turkey's first president, and crossed the narrow stretch of water called the Golden Horn that connected with the Bosporous Strait.

There were so many things to see Nancy craned her neck this way and that so as not to miss anything. Since it was noon, the streets were crowded with businessmen, shoppers, and foreign visitors.

"I notice there is a preponderance of men," Nancy remarked. "Also that some of the peasant women wear traditional long black skirts and head scarves drawn over their faces.

Aisha said that while Turkey was now western in its thinking, and has adopted the clothes, and business and banking methods of Europe, many of the old customs remain.

"One of these is that married women stay in their homes a great part of the time. Later on you will probably see some of them in the mosques. They usually come in groups."

Aisha directed their driver to two estates on the

outskirts of the city. The taxi carrying their companions pulled up behind. Mr Hatun got out and went inside with Mr Drew and the boys. He returned in a few minutes and this taxi followed the other.

Presently they entered a gateway which was part of a highly ornamented iron fence. They went past lovely gardens with a profusion of roses and finally came to a large house. The architecture was like that of old Greece – an oblong building of smooth stone fronted with many columns.

The group got out. Aisha and her mother led the way to the massive front door. They used the knocker once and the door was opened by a servant wearing traditional Turkish uniform. He bowed low.

As the man walked off to announce the newcomers to his master and mistress, Bess grabbed Nancy's hand and whispered, "Oh, isn't it romantic! I'm so glad we didn't have to go to a hotel!"

In a few minutes their host and his wife came in. They were wearing simple Western-style daytime clothes. Aisha introduced them as Mr and Mrs Hrozny, old friends.

The couple shook hands and apologized for not speaking English very well. Mr Hrozny said, "We are happy to have you come. We hope you will enjoy your visit." His eyes twinkled. "Which is the young lady with the mystery?"

Aisha presented Nancy. Then in turn she introduced Bess and George.

After the visitors had freshened up, they enjoyed a delicious luncheon. It consisted of rice sprinkled with bits of lamb and served with a curry sauce. This was followed by small bowls of fruit with grapes, figs, and dates. A pink custard sauce had been poured over the fruit.

A short time later, Mr and Mrs Hatun said they must start for home. When they had driven off, Aisha said, "Mr and Mrs Hrozny have engaged a small bus to take all of us sightseeing. As soon as you girls are ready, we will pick up the boys and start our tour."

She smiled. "I suppose the biggest clue to finding Farouk is the shoeshine stand. I do not know exactly where any are but we'll look around the bazaars."

The bus driver was young and very handsome. Bess whispered to George and Nancy, "This place is so full of good-looking men, it's fortunate I have a date of my own or I'd be tempted to accept an invitation from one of these Turkish boys."

"Better not let Dave hear you say that," George advised. "Unless you pick out a *man*-nequin." The others giggled.

They picked up the boys at the Kokten home and started their tour. Mr Drew went off to call on a law school acquaintance. The sightseers crossed the Ataturk Bridge once more and went directly to one of the mosques.

"This is called the Suleymaniye Mosque," Aisha said. "We will not go inside, but I brought you here to show you something I'm sure you have never seen in your country. The Koran states that anyone entering the mosque must have clean feet. There are several places outside the building for foot bathing."

There was a park at one side of the building. In it stood a small circular section depressed below the ground. There was a ledge all the way round for men to sit on. Below the ledge were faucets of water. Further on, hugging the side of the mosque, was a row of faucets with benches to sit on and bathe one's feet. Nearly all of them were filled.

"Now all these men will go inside and pray," Aisha said. "You know Moslems pray five times a day."

The visitors left the park and the bus took them to the outskirts of the Grand Bazaar. Aisha explained that the shops in it paid rent to the Blue Mosque. Excitedly the group walked towards the huge conglomerate of shops under one vast roof. Just before entering it, Nancy grabbed Ned's arm.

"A shoeshine stand!"

In front of a building stood the ornate object with colourful tile insets depicting old-time scenes. Apparently they had been taken from Turkish legend and were framed in a rectangle of gold. On either side of it were golden winglike projections that glistened in the sun.

The shoeshine man sat behind it cross-legged. He smiled at the group. On impulse Nancy decided to ask him if he spoke English. If so, she would inquire if he knew Mr Farouk Tahmasp.

As she approached the shoeshine man, he stood up, waved his arms wildly, and cried out, "*Yok! Yok!*"

Nancy was puzzled. She asked Aisha what *Yok* meant and was told, "an emphatic no." The Turkish girl spoke to the man, then translated. "He thinks you want to have your shoes shined, but says he never shines a woman's shoes on her feet."

The young people smiled at the misunderstanding and Nancy said, "I don't want my shoes shined. I was merely going to ask if he knows Farouk."

The shoeshine man said he had never served nor heard of Farouk Tahmasp. While they were talking, George noticed a young man running towards them.

She turned to the Turkish girl and asked, "Aisha, is this Farouk coming?"

The girl looked. For a few seconds she did not reply. The others watched tensely. Finally the man drew closer and Aisha shook her head. A look of disappointment crossed her face.

Bess put an arm over the girl's shoulders. "Cheer up, Aisha," she said. "We'll find him yet."

The Turkish girl said nothing and led the way into the bazaar. The din was deafening! Bells jangled. Hawkers called out their wares, ranging from copper cooking utensils to leather luggage. Crowds of people, mostly Turkish men and tourists, milled along the narrow streets. Dogs roamed at will. The whole area was well-lighted by unshaded electric bulbs in many of the open-front shops, particularly where men were urging passers-by to purchase their jewellery. There were markets with cuts of lamb and dried fish hanging up, and bakeries with baklava and other pastries.

The travellers rambled on. They decided to keep close together, because there were so many people coming and going that one could easily become separated from the group. But every now and then one of them would pause to look at the various articles for sale and would have to catch up with the others.

Aisha became concerned and requested that they all stayed with the group. After walking several blocks, she came to a halt.

"You say in your country you count noses," she said, smiling. "I will now count your noses."

Bess was not with them.

"Did anyone see her?" Dave asked, worried.

"Not lately," they all admitted.

Dave said nervously, "She was right beside me back there a little ways. I'll go and look for her."

"We will all go," said Aisha.

They peered into every shop as they retraced their steps. Bess was not in any of them nor was she on the street. Her friends became genuinely alarmed.

Bazaar Kidnapping

About fifteen minutes before the search for Bess had begun, she had been intrigued by a perfume shop on a street corner in the bazaar.

The owner peered from the doorway at her. "Come in, lady," he invited. "I give you free sample."

As a mixture of delightful scents drifted outside, Bess said to herself, "The place smells heavenly. If his perfumes are this good, I really should buy some to take home."

She stepped inside. There were shelves on three sides of the room filled with large bottles. On a counter stood dozens of small glass flacons encased in gold filigree.

"You pick," the man said to Bess. "I put perfume in bottle."

He took down several of the large jars and with a long rod began to daub various scents on Bess's arms.

"Which you like?" the shopkeeper asked.

Many of the scents smelled like spices mixed with flowers. Bess like them all and could not make up her mind which one to buy.

"They're all lovely," she said, sniffing at one bottle, then another.

Meanwhile the man reached under the counter and brought out a midget-sized bottle of perfume. He handed it to Bess. "My compliments to lady from the the United States," he said, bowing. "You will like."

Bess giggled as she thanked him. "And I think I will buy this scent," she said, pointing to an area on one arm just below her elbow.,

"Very good taste," the perfume dealer remarked. "Very good indeed."

For the firt time Bess became aware of the man's looks. He was tall and slender and had very white skin. He wore a tiny moustache and his hair was dark and wavy.

"You are Turkish?" she asked.

The shopkeeper smiled. "I am half Turkish, half French. My father – he is perfume maker in France. I learned from him."

"Do you make all these kinds yourself?" Bess inquired.

"Yes."

He pourd out the scent Bess had chosen into a gold filigree bottle. Before he finished, a boy of about seventeen came into the shop. He addressed himself to Bess.

"Pardon, mademoiselle. I was sent to tell you your party is waiting."

"Oh, thank you," said Bess. She told the perfume dealer she would be back to buy more perfume, paid for her purchase, and started from the shop.

"I show you where your party is," the boy said.

For the first time Bess realized she had been in the

perfume store for some time. Presently her escort pointed up a side street. "Your party in shop there. Come!"

Bess hurried along after him. It seemed like a long way up the covered street of the bazaar. Finally he stopped before a display of Turkish rugs behind an iron grillwork.

Suddenly Bess became suspicious. She did not see her friends anywhere.

The boy must have guessed her thoughts because he said, "Your party look at pictures in back room and talk to man."

Bess craned her neck and thought she saw George's back. It occurred to her that Nancy had investigated the rug shop and perhaps had found Farouk! As she stepped into the outer room of the shop, her escort slammed the iron grating doorway shut and locked it. Grabbing the key, he called to someone in the rear room in Turkish.

Bess was terrified. She wanted to scream but not a sound came from her throat. She had been deliberately trapped. But why? And who was behind it?

A moment later she found out. A young man came to the outer room. He looked at Bess, gave a low sardonic chuckle, then said, "You are here because of your friend Nancy Drew. You will be prisoner of my family until I get treasure hidden inside the mannequin belonging to Farouk Tahmasp."

Bess was shaking like a leaf but she managed to stutter, "I – I don't know anything about a treasure and we didn't find the mannequin. What do you want with me?"

The man stared at Bess a long time as if he did not know whether to believe her or not. Finally he shrugged. "It does not matter. You will stay here until I get it!"

Bess was in a panic. She must escape. But how?

Just then a woman appeared and escorted her into the rear room. The only other person there was a little girl of about ten, who was evidently her child. On a table in one corner stood a telephone. The older man pointed to it.

"Telephone Nancy Drew and tell her to meet you at the big hotel on the hill."

Bess's heart leapt for joy. She figured that the man had had a change of heart and soon would let her go free since she did not know where the mannequin or the treasure was.

"Say nothing more than what I told you," the man directed.

He handed Bess a telephone book and after a struggle she found the number of the Hrozny house. She pointed it out to the man who put in the call. As soon as someone answered, he motioned to Bess to reply.

To her delight Dave was on the other end. If only she could tell him what had happened! But she did not dare. She gave him the message exactly as she had been told.

"Where are you? What happended?" Dave replied in bewilderment. "I've been worried about you."

Bess glanced at her captor and repeated the message, then he put down the phone.

Deeply worried about his date's whereabouts, Dave waited impatiently for one of the others in the group to call. It had been arranged that he would hurry to the Hrozny house on a chance that Bess, having become separated from the rest of the group, might have returned there.

Nancy was to telephone later to find out. In the meantime they would continue the search in the bazaar. Bess's friends queried various shopkeepers and some American tourists, but none of them had seen a girl fitting Bess's description. Her friends became more and more alarmed.

Aisha had gone off to make some inquiries in her native tongue, hoping for some clue to Bess's whereabouts. She returned to report a vain search also.

"It's about time to call Dave," said Nancy. "Aisha, where will we find a phone?"

The Turkish girl led her into a shop that sold all kinds of leather goods — saddles, riding boots, purses and luggage. Aisha made the call. Nancy was relieved when she saw a smile break over the girl's face.

"Bess is home?" she asked as Aisha put down the phone.

"No, but she wants to meet you at the big hotel overlooking the city. I suppose she didn't know the name of it." Suddenly a look of concern crossed the girl's face. "Dave said Bess gave no explanation for her disappearance — just repeated the message."

"That's not like Bess," said Nancy.

"What if she's in trouble!" George remarked fearfully.

"I know the bazaar is crowded and it's easy to become separated," Nancy put in, "but we weren't walking very fast and I don't see why Bess couldn't have caught up with us easily. I'm terribly worried about her."

Burt frowned. "Do you think the phone call Dave took could have been a hoax?"

"Not necessarily," Nancy replied. "But someone may have forced her to make it. I haven't any idea who would want to kidnap Bess or why. If Bess is really at the hotel I'll be the most relieved person in the world."

It was a pretty sombre group that made its way by taxis through the city and up the hill to the attractive hotel that overlooked the city and its beautiful harbour. Nancy and her friends quickly alighted from the taxis and went into the spacious lobby. Bess Marvin was not in sight.

"Just as I suspected," Nancy thought.

Dave arrived in a few minutes. "Is she here?" he asked quickly.

"No."

The distraught boy began pacing the floor nervously. "Where is she?" He caught the worried expresssion on the faces of the others. "Has something happened that I don't know about? Tell me."

Nancy said, "It's only a hunch – and I hope I'm wrong – but I'm afraid Bess is being held prisoner somewhere and won't come."

"Then why did she ask you to meet her here?" Dave wanted to know.

"We may get another message," Nancy answered. "I think that as long as we all stay together, there is not much likelihood of a messenger coming to me. I suggest that you all scatter and hide in advantageous places. If a stranger does come to talk to me or deliver a note, you boys follow him. Please."

The young people sauntered off and disappeared from view, some inside the building, the rest outside.

Fifteen minutes went by. Nancy, seated in a chair facing the entrance to the hotel, had just begun to wonder if her theory was wrong, when a boy of about seventeen approached her. He bowed politely.

"Pardon, mademoiselle. I have seen pictures of you. You are Miss Nancy Drew from River Heights of USA?"

"Yes."

"Someone admires you very much. He asked me to bring a message."

From his shabby pocket he pulled a small letter. With another little bow he handed it to Nancy, then without saying goodbye hurried off.

Nancy jumped up, her suspicions thoroughly aroused. She did not wait to read the letter. Instead she spotted Ned near a pillar and quickly gave him the high sign to follow the boy. She herself hurried out the door. George was at her heels.

"Who is he?" she asked Nancy.

The young detective did not reply. She had seen a

man emerge from a taxi and go after the Turkish boy. She recognized him.

"George!" cried Nancy. "That's Aslanapa! I'll bet he saw us. He's going to warn that messenger he'll be followed and not to reveal where Bess is hidden!"

·19·

An Arrest

Aslanapa was fleet-footed, but before he could overtake the messenger, he apparently realized that Ned, Burt, and Dave were after the boy. The bearded, moustached suspect suddenly turned and went down the side street.

A traffic policeman stood on the corner. Aisha spoke to him, briefly telling him that one of their party might have been kidnapped. "We think that the man we were chasing may be the guilty person." At once the officer began running with the girls.

"There he goes!" George cried out. "Into that garden!"

The pursuers rushed in after him and the officer found the man, crouched down, hiding behind some low-growing evergreens.

"He's the one all right!" Nancy said, seeing a gold filigree bracelet studded with turquoise on one arm. "His name is Aslanapa."

The suspect, realizing he was cornered, was silent.

Nancy went on, "Officer, I accuse this man of having entered my home in the United States and of trying to steal a special rug made here in Istanbul.

Later he came back and left a scimitar to frighten me."

George spoke. "He was making scimitars and master keys to sell without license and was wanted by the police in the United States."

Nancy added, "One of the girls in our group has disappeared. We think he is holding her somewhere, probably for ransom."

Remembering the note in her pocket, she read it quickly and said, "Here is a message ordering me to give information about a treasure secreted in a mannequin. Otherwise my kidnapped friend will not be released."

Aslanapa panicked and tried to climb over a garden wall near him. But the officer dragged him back and held on tightly.

"I will request my superior to send a police car," the officer said. "Please to watch the prisoner."

Nancy and George moved closer to Aslanapa while the policeman used his short-wave radio to call headquarters.

Aslanapa's face was livid. His eyes bored into Nancy's as he said, "You can prove nothing against me!"

Just then they saw a police car coming up the street. The policeman marched Aslanapa out the garden and the others followed. At the same time a taxi pulled up. In it were Bess, Ned, Burt, and Dave!

"Bess!" George shrieked.

The young people got out of the taxi and Ned paid the driver.

"You're all right?" George asked her cousin.

"I am now," Bess replied. Then she caught sight of the prisoner. Quickly Nancy told her who he was.

"Aslanapa!" Bess cried out. Pointing a finger at him, she added, "You're the one who engineered my kidnapping!"

"Tell us about it," Nancy begged.

The traffic officer said he must return to his post. The two who had come in the police car would take care of the prisoner.

At her friends urging, Bess told of the kidnapping. "The boy who lied to me about where you all had gone and locked me in is Aslanapa's brother. He came back to the place after delivering the letter to you, Nancy.

"I told the people at the rug shop I had never heard of such a treasure and that we hadn't found the mannequin," Bess went on, "but they didn't believe me. I wondered how long I would have to stay."

Bess looked gratefully at the three boys. "Just when I was feeling about as low as I could," she said, "Aslanapa's brother returned. When he unlocked the door and let himself in, Dave, Burt and Ned jumped on him. Dave grabbed my hand and said, 'Come on!' and we all ran like mad out of that bazaar."

The two officers wrote down the names of Bess and Nancy and requested that they come to police headquarters at once.

"Where are we going to find your dad?" Ned asked. "I'd say we need the services of a lawyer."

Aisha offered to telephone the Kokten home. Fortunately Mr Drew was there and amazed at what had taken place.

"I'll come directly to police headquarters."

The others had to wait a short while for him. When he came, Aisha smiled at Mr Drew. "There are many legal problems when a foreign tourist is involved," she said. "I am so glad that you are an attorney."

The Turkish authorities expressed embarrassment that one of their countrymen had abducted an American citizen and acted so badly in the United States. Aslanapa and his family had been arrested. The officers hurried with the necessary procedures so Bess and the Drews could leave. By the time they were over, everyone in the group, including Mr Drew, was starving.

"Let's go back to that lovely hotel and have lunch," Nancy proposed.

They walked to it and ate heartily while discussing the latest events in the mystery. After the serious subjects had been discussed, Bess came in for plenty of teasing including a gibe from Burt that of all the pretty girls in Istanbul, Aslanapa had to pick her to take into his family! She made a face at Burt.

George grinned,. "You had your wish. You met a handsome Turkish man!"

During the exchange of banter Nancy noticed that while Aisha smiled at the jokes, she had a sort of sweet-sad expression.

"Her mind is on Farouk," Nancy thought. "I must help her!"

Presently she called to Aisha, "Are you redy for some more sightseeing? We'll look for shoeshine stands and rug shops to see if we can locate Farouk."

"That would be wonderful," the Turkish girl replied. "But first I want to take you to the Blue Mosque."

Aisha managed to locate the private bus in which they had started the morning's sightseeing trip. When it arrived, they all boarded it and the driver went directly to the Blue Mosque.

"See the seven domes framed by those tall spires?" Aisha said. "The sultan who built them kept adding one after another so that he would always be ahead of any other sultan. No one ever matched the number seven."

At the main door the visitors removed their shoes. It was dim in the interior but presently their eyes became accustomed to it. At the far end of the mosque, men were on their knees, their foreheads close to the floor. They were praying.

Some distance behind them was a group of Turkish women in the same position. They wore long black dresses with full sleeves that covered their arms completely and their large black veils entirely hid their hair and faces.

"The women are not allowed to go up front until the men leave," Aisha explained.

The visitors stood still, looking up at the exquisite arched ceiling, with its mosaic pattern, much of it in gold. The boys were awed by the electric candles which were seventy-seven feet high.

Nancy was intrigued by the gorgeous prayer rugs that lay on the floor around her. There was enough light from the doorway for her to study the pattern in one of them. A moment later she saw something that excited her.

She whispered to Aisha, "In that rug, part of the pattern looks like marble columns rising out of water."

As Aisha nodded, Nancy said, "In the rug that Farouk sent there was something like that. I admit, I didn't think it had any significance, but maybe it does."

"Oh, I believe it does," Aisha said. "It could indicate the Great Cistern."

"Where's that?" Nancy asked.

Aisha said it was in Istanbul. They would go there at once. "It might mean the place where Farouk was going to meet us!"

She motioned to the others to leave the mosque. When they were in the bus once more, she directed the driver to take them to the Great Cistern. Aisha explained that it was an enormous underground reservoir and had been built in the fourth century by Constantine the Great.

"At that time there was much jealousy among the sultans and nations and wars were going on. The sultan in Istanbul was afraid the city might be besieged, and though the people could hold out for a long time behind the great wall, if they did not have water to drink, they would die. Water coming into it underground could not be cut off by the enemy. The cistern was enlarged in the sixth century by the Emperor Justinian."

Despite Aisha's interesting story, the others were not prepared for the tremendous sight they found at the foot of a stone stairway. The place was like a gigantic swimming pool with columns rising from the bottom to the floor of the building above it.

"Wow!" Burt exclaimed. "There's enough water in here to keep a whole army from getting thirsty!"

Aisha smiled. "I understand that in olden days the water was deeper. It's rather shallow now. You might be interested in the dimensions of this place. It's four hundred and twenty by two hundred feet and it has three hundred and thirty-six columns."

"Is it still used?" Nancy asked, going to the edge and looking down into the clear water.

"No, not any more. But in an emergency I suppose it could be."

Ned remarked about the ceiling which was fluted and arched between columns. The others looked up.

Everyone was so intent on the exquisite architecture that they failed to notice a figure slinking towards them. Quick as a flash he came up behind Nancy and gave her a hard push.

She tumbled into the cistern and hit the side of her head on the bottom!

Mission Accomplished

There were cries of dismay as Nancy's friends realized she had hit her head. Like a flash Ned was in the water to rescue her. When he finally brought Nancy out, she appeared dazed.

"Oh," wailed Bess, "we'd better take her to a hospital at once!"

Meanwhile Burt and Dave had run after the boy who had pushed Nancy into the Great Cistern. They caught him at the top of the stairway and dragged him back to the group. He struggled violently, threatening them in both Turkish and English.

In the dim light the Americans had not recognized the boy, but the instant Bess saw him she cried out, "Aslanapa's brother Mustafa! The one who lured me to the shop!"

Mustafa glared at the group. "Nancy Drew deserved what she got. She had no right to put my brother in jail!"

By this time Nancy was sitting up on the floor. She declared there was no need for her to go to a hospital or even to see a doctor.

"I guess the water broke the full impact of my fall,"

she said. "I did hit my head and I'll have some black-and-blue marks, but I'm sure I'll be all right."

She rubbed the side of her head vigorously to pep up the circulation.

Presently she looked up at the boy prisoner. "You know as well as I do that your brother had no right to kidnap my friend. You are what we call in our country an accessory after the fact, but I don't know what the law here is in such cases." She looked up at her father. "Do you, Dad?"

"No, I don't," he admitted. "Right now I'm more concerned about you than these lawbreakers. The police will have to deal with them. I suggest that Burt and Dave and Aisha take this boy directly to head-quarters. The rest of us will drive back to where we're staying. By that time, Nancy, you will know how you feel. You'll want to shower and put on fresh clothes. Ned too."

Nancy stood up and they walked towards the stairway. Coming down was a handsome young man. Seeing them, he rushed forward.

The next moment Aisha cried out, "Farouk!"

She leapt forward to meet him and the two embraced. The others held back to give Aisha and Farouk a chance to talk privately.

Bess was in ecstasy. "They found each other!" she said happily. "Oh, what a wonderful ending to the mystery!"

George reminded her that one angle of the mystery had not yet been solved — that of the mysterious mannequin.

"But it will be soon," Bess insisted.

"I've been wondering," said Nancy, "how Farouk knew we were down here."

At that moment Aisha brought her fiancé over to introduce him. He bowed and said, "My hopes have been realized. Every day I have been passing the shoeshine stands in this vicinity and coming down here since I mailed the rug to Mr Drew! I knew that one day Aisha and I would find each other. I understand I have every one of you to thank for this reunion. Mr Drew, I want to apologize for running away. I was frightened of being sent to one of your American prisons, even though I was innocent. I should have had more faith in the justice of your courts."

Aisha spoke up. "I have told Farouk that he was proved innocent."

"That's right," Mr Drew agreed. "The trouble about the smuggling charge started over here in Turkey. It was a case of mistaken identity."

Farouk looked gratefully at the lawyer, then put an arm round Aisha. "Now we can marry," he said.

Aisha smiled happily and said, "Would you all mind if Farouk and I spend a little time together and meet you later?"

Mr Drew nodded. "We wouldn't have it any other way. I shall reserve a big table for dinner in the roof restaurant of the hotel that you like. Then we can exchange stories. Shall we say eight o'clock?"

Everyone accepted the invitation, but to herself Bess was saying, "I can never last until eight o'clock without food. But maybe I can find something at the Hroznys' house."

Her hunger problem was solved by their hostess when she invited them all to assemble in the garden for a five-o'clock tea hour.

After Nancy had bathed and rested for a while, she insisted that she felt fine and her unexpected dip in the Great Cistern had not really harmed her.

While they were eating Mrs Hrozny's pastries, most of them sweetened with honey and filled with nuts and dates, and drinking the delicious tea from the Black Sea area, the girls brought her up to date on the mystery.

"Isn't it romantic the way Aisha found Farouk, or shall I say Farouk found Aisha!" Bess exclaimed.

The Turkish woman smiled. "I am happy for Aisha. She is a brave girl. It was very hard for her to be parted from Farouk."

George mentioned the dinner plans for the evening. Mrs Hrozny smiled. "Mr Drew has already telephoned and extended an invitation to my husband and me. He has also invited our friends the Koktens."

"I'm glad," said Nancy. "You have had a part in this mystery too."

Mr Drew had engaged a private dining room. A long table had been set up. A beautiful bouquet of roses stood in the centre with trailing vines of ivy reaching all the way down to each end.

Aisha and Farouk were the last to arrive. Both appeared in colourful costume. He wore satin knee-breeches, long socks, and fancy shoes with curled-up toes. On his head was an ornamented turban such as sultans used to wear.

Aisha had on pale-blue pantaloons, slippers with curled-up toes, and a cerise blouse. Wound round her head and across her face, with only her eyes showing, was a white scarf, which she removed before sitting down.

Everyone clapped and there were compliments of "You look beautiful!" "You look handsome!"

The happy couple smiled and Aisha said, "We thought these costumes might be appropriate for the occasion. We wanted to show you how grateful we are that the mystery is solved."

Mr Drew had arranged place cards, putting himself at one end with Mrs Hrozny at his right and on his left Mrs Kokten. Nancy was assigned to the other end of the table with Mr Hrozny on her right and Mr Kokten on her left. The rest of the guests were seated in between, with the bride and groom-to-be facing the centre of the table on one side.

During the dinner there was lively chatter among the guests, but as soon as desert had been finished, Farouk stood up.

"I want to take this opportunity of thanking everyone again. Through you our prayers were answered." He turned and looked directly at Nancy. "You were the prime mover in bringing Aisha here. After I fled, I realized I would never be happy until she was with me. But I saw no chance of this. I did not dare communicate with her. I am descended from a long line of proud people, the Tahmasps. However, I wanted to tell where I was hiding and thought up the idea of the rug."

He smiled. "Mr Drew seemed like the logical person to whom to send it and he could tell me how my case came out. He is a very good lawyer and then I had heard his daughter is an excellent amateur detective. I thought she could work out through the words and symbols in the rug where I could be found."

At that there were cheers and clapping for half a minute.

Farouk sat down. When the applause had died down, George called out, "One part of the mystery has not been solved. Will you please tell us where the mannequin is and if there is a treasure hidden in her."

Farouk and Aisha exchanged glances, then Aisha stood up. Her eyes were twinkling as she said, "I am going to ask Nancy to tell you. She worked it out some time ago and spoke to me about it one day when we went for a drive. I admitted she was right and asked that she keep the secret until we had Farouk's permission to reveal it."

As Aisha sat down, Nancy got up. She glanced at her Turkish friend, who gave her a wink. "Aisha was the mannequin!"

Nancy's friends looked at the young detective in utter astonishment. Finally Ned said, "How in the world did you figure that out?"

Nancy said that her suspicions had been aroused by her recollection that about six years go she was sure that the mannequin had winked at her.

"Even though I went back to the shop window and

stared at her several times and she never blinked, I could not get it out of my mind. Then I learned from neighbours that the mannequin was never in the window for long periods. This seemed a little strange to me and I began to wonder if it was because she might be a real person and therefore unable to pose for long at a time.

"You recall the slippers that were under the trap door in the back of the shop? They definitely indicated someone had walked in them but not far. I figured that perhaps the mannequin walked through the shop. Then Farouk would lift her up on to the bench and cover her lap with a rug. By the way, Aisha hid her costume under the trap door. When Farouk took it away he forgot the slippers."

Nancy smiled. "I was puzzled as to why Farouk could love a mannequin so much that he would want her brought from America to Turkey. Of course it might have been because he had hidden jewels or something else in her. But taking her abroad would not be feasible. Custom officials would be sure to find anything secreted."

Nancy's listeners were dumbfounded. Finally Ned spoke up, "One day when we were on a trip up the river you sketched an imaginary picture of the mannequin's face. I didn't pay much attention to it except to notice she was very beautiful. Did you think she looked like Aisha?"

Nancy laughed. "Only the eyes."

"You are amazing," Mr Hrozny said.

Everyone clapped and called out compliments to

Nancy as she sat down. When it was quiet again, George turned to Farouk, "Please don't keep me in suspense any longer. Was there or was there not a treasure involved?"

Once again Farouk got up. "In a way, there was. Aisha became my mannequin to help protect it."

The young Turkish rug dealer went on to say that many people came to his shop and brought cash. Often it amounted to a thousand dollars. His listeners gasped.

"No doubt I was foolish," Farouk said, "not to put the money in a bank. Several times I had been robbed of small amounts of money. One of the thieves was Aslanapa. I know he suspected I had large sums around. It was then that I arranged for Aisha to keep the money in her clothes while she was posing as a mannequin. Fortunately no one ever suspected our secret. When I left I had to flee the United States, I sewed all the money in my own clothing and brought it with me.

At that point Mr Drew took an envelope from his pocket, left his chair, and came over to Farouk's side.

"You left money with me to pay for my services," he said. "It was far too much. I am glad now to deliver it to you." He smiled. "Maybe you will want to use it for a memento to put in your new home."

Farouk insisted it should be used to pay for the lawyer's trip to Istanbul, but Mr Drew would not hear of this. "You keep it."

Aisha spoke up. "The most wonderful memento we

could have would be a fine painting of all you people who helped to solve the mystery."

The mere mention of the word mystery quickened Nancy's pulse, and filled her mind with questions. What would her next adventure be? Would it take her far from home? Her questions were answered a few days later when she was asked to investigate another puzzling case, *The Crooked Banister*.

It was only Farouk's next remark that jolted the pretty detective back to the present. "In this painting I want Nancy Drew to have the place of honour in the middle for having brought my mannequin to me."